Skins

SARAH HAY was born in Esperance, Western Australia, in 1966. A journalist and public relations consultant, she began her career as a cadet livestock reporter in Perth. She has worked in England as a reporter for a national newspaper. She has also been a writer for two public relations firms in Perth. Currently an undergraduate at the University of Western Australia, she is completing a Bachelor of Arts in English and Philosophy and writing her second novel. She lives in Perth with her husband and son.

SARAH HAY

ALLEN&UNWIN

First published in 2002

 This project has been assisted by the Commonwealth
Government through the Australia Council, its arts funding
and advisory body.

Allen & Unwin
83 Alexander Street
Crows Nest NSW 2065
Australia
Phone: (61 2) 8425 0100
Fax: (61 2) 9906 2218
Email: info@allenandunwin.com
Web: www.allenandunwin.com

National Library of Australia
Cataloguing-in-Publication entry:

Hay, Sarah, 1966–.
   Skins.

   ISBN 1 86508 807 2.

   1. Aborigines, Australian—Women—Western Australia—History.
   2. Sealers (Persons)—Western Australia—History.
   3. Aborigines, Australian—Western Australia—History. I. Title.

305.4889915

Set in 11.5pt on 14pt Adobe Garamond by Asset Typesetting Pty Ltd

10 9 8 7 6 5 4 3 2 1

For my family

Acknowledgements

I owe much to my parents Ian and Jan Hay for choosing to live in a special and remote part of Western Australia. This book could not have been written without the help of John Cahill who accompanied me on my trips to Middle Island.

CSIRO's Dr Peter Shaughnessy and Dr Nick Gales, who is now with the Australian Antarctic Division, shared their knowledge of sea lions and fur seals on a research trip to Kangaroo Island. Malcolm Traill and Julia Mitchell from the Local Studies Section of the Albany Library were always helpful in their responses to my numerous enquiries.

My thanks to Marcella Pollain and Dr Brenda Walker of the University of Western Australia's creative writing program for getting me started and Brenda for reading my completed manuscript.

Thanks to my grandmother Nancy Hay who read my chapters as they were written and for her belief in my work; my friends Kerry and Garry Walker for our Friday night discussions that helped me discover what I wanted to say; my husband Jamie Venerys for his support; Chris and Christine Bradley; Jill Bear; Stephen and Dorothy Purdew; and my son Robert for being there.

January 1886

Do you remember the island that lay in the middle of others? Rocks washed smooth by the sea. How frightened we were? But it was only the beginning. I am so tired now and there is a coldness inside me that is spreading.

Middle Island 1835, James Manning

Manning didn't consider himself one of Anderson's men. It was nearly two years since he had left the settled shores of Sydney Town for the new Swan River colony, a journey of some three and a half thousand nautical miles. That didn't take into account the detours they would make to the sealers' camps hidden on small rocky islands that broke the surge of the Southern Ocean swell. But Manning never reached the Swan River colony. He had left Botany Bay as part of the crew of a sealing trader called the *Defiance* but the schooner was wrecked off the coast of New South Wales. Some of the crew had taken the longboat back to Sydney. He and the others had gone on in the whaleboat to Kangaroo Island. It was there he met the sealer Black Jack Anderson.

Manning was sitting halfway up the sandhill that followed the curve of the main bay at Middle Island. It was called Goose Island Bay, named after the island that lay off its shore about one and a half miles to the west and which sheltered it from the Southern Ocean swell.

He watched a solitary seagull flap against the wind above the beach. It gave up and glided down and out across the dark foam-flecked sea. As it neared the tip of the waves, it flapped again, turning in a wide arc before it headed back to the beach, perhaps knowing that if it left the island, it would have to fend for itself instead of relying on the scraps left by the sealers. Manning thought if he was a bird, he would take his chances. He could see the purple hills of Mount Arid that was the mainland, six miles away. He would stretch out his wings and let the wind carry him there. No longer to be buffeted by the gusts that came up and over the island from the land of ice in the south. Manning threw out a piece of stale crust. He was tired of chewing the hard bread that stuck in his throat when he swallowed. The little gull swooped with its feet poised to take it. A black-winged Pacific gull came out of the sky and, just as the silver gull lifted the crust off the ground, the big gull snatched the bread and carried it up and over the sandhills.

Today was the 27th of March 1835. Manning knew that because he had scratched eighty-six notches on the stick he kept beside his swag to mark every day since he had arrived. He had come to Middle Island with Anderson from Kangaroo Island, on the promise the sealer would take him on to King George Sound. And from there to Swan River would be easy. But Anderson was a hard bastard, making him work for his food. Manning knew that if they didn't leave soon it would be much later in the year before the winds would be favourable again. He also knew that if he didn't get up from where he was sitting soon, Anderson would be after him.

But Anderson would always be after him. A gust of wind sent pricks of sand across his face. He picked up a handful and watched it trickle through his fist. It made him think of time passing but that was strange for since he had been on the island he had felt as though it stood still. It was very fine sand and white like snow, perhaps. He looked up, his chin resting on his knees. Suddenly he saw something on the horizon. Could it be a sail? He stood up, brushing the sand from his ragged trousers, and squinted into the distance, motionless for a moment, his eyes fixed on that point. The swell had been whipped up by a storm a couple of nights ago. Now the wind had swung around to the east and was blowing hard across the bay. It was difficult to see through the salt haze, which hovered above the white-capped waves. But yes it was the sail of a small boat. He expected to see a ship further out but there was no sign of one. He kept watching the boat as he came down the hill and along the beach. He reached the granite beyond the camp which was tucked in behind the sand dunes. Once he rounded the head-land he lost sight of the sail and Goose Island blocked his view of the mainland. He continued west along a short beach littered with clumps of brown seaweed. He climbed over boulders and small rocks to reach another bay. This time he faced the massive granite dome of Flinders Peak, which stood on the north-western corner of the island. The sun came out from behind a cloud and intensified the orange and brown stripes that ran down the purple rock face.

Anderson's whaleboat was pulled up at the foot of the sandhill and lay tilted to one side. Usually they brought their catch to the main beach but today Anderson had taken his boat around to the other side because it was sheltered. Away from the wind the sun was hot on the back of Manning's neck. A tripot rested on a ring of granite boulders. As he passed by, he felt the heat from the coals on his legs. Dinah was placing slabs of quivering white fat into the pot and stirring, her skin shiny with sweat. Anderson's other woman Sal, who was shorter and broader, squatted a short distance away and used a wooden paddle to scrape the fat from a skin pulled tight over a rock.

He walked into the smoke and the thick stench caught the back of his throat. He reached Anderson and his men at the water's edge. Seals were laid out on the sand like giant slugs. The men sliced and peeled the skin from the carcasses, widening the red stain around them. Their knives flashed as they caught the light. They brought them under the neck and down the belly to the tail, turning the seal over to take the fat and the skin from its back. And then the hide was turned inside out over the flippers like clothing being removed. Squawking gulls swooped and fought between them. Anderson looked up.

'Soger,' he growled at Manning.

He straightened, unfolding the full strength of his black body, which was barely clad in seal and kangaroo skin, looking for the pail of fresh water Manning was to have brought with him. Both hands were bloodied. A piece of dirty cloth was tied around his forehead to prevent the sweat from entering his eyes.

Before he could say anything else, Manning said: 'There's a boat.'

They stopped and looked out towards the channel between the islands but they couldn't see anything.

'Who is it?'

Manning shrugged, looking down at the ground. Anderson wiped his knife and put it away and walked towards the sandhill. He gestured for Manning to follow. They climbed the steep hill to the track through the dense bush to the camp so that they wouldn't be seen from the sea. It was hot inland. Thin scraggly trees lined the pathway and dead foliage lay amongst the undergrowth. Sticks cracked beneath their feet. Soon they reached a large area of granite that was almost completely surrounded by bush. A short track led to Anderson's hut. Anderson disappeared through the doorway and returned with his musket.

The whaleboat glided into the bay on the stiff breeze. There were nine people on board and it was low in the water. As it came closer, they could see that two of them were women. From the helm there was a shout and a man stood up, waving his right arm.

'Oy! Anderson!'

Anderson gave no sign he knew him. But Manning knew that he did. It was Evanson Jansen, the captain of a sealer trader Anderson had paid in skins to bring him and his men to Middle Island. Jansen's cutter the *Mountaineer* had left Kangaroo Island fully laden with Anderson's whaleboat, skins, supplies and men, as well as Manning, and had dumped them all on the beach only three months earlier. Manning wondered what had happened to the *Mountaineer*. And it was clear that Anderson wasn't expecting its captain. Manning knew no sealer liked an unexpected visitor, no matter how well he knew him. Anderson stood, legs apart, holding the musket in one hand.

Manning stared hard at the women, realising that he hadn't seen the skin of a white woman for nearly two years. Their faces were pale, framed in tatty bonnets. The men leapt from the boat into the clear green shallows, some of them too soon since in parts it was too deep to stand. They splashed through the icy water and waited for the swell to propel the boat forward. Then they heaved it up onto the beach.

Anderson stood over the men who surrounded him. He held the gun across his body, the end of the barrel resting in his left hand. Manning saw Jansen glance uneasily at it and then clear his throat. Manning knew Anderson well enough to know he was angry. The sealer had made Jansen promise not to reveal his whereabouts to anyone and had given the man his best skins to keep him quiet. But Jansen had brought strangers to Anderson's camp. Manning recognised two of the crew from the trip over. And there was also another man who seemed familiar but he wasn't sure why. The others he had never seen before.

⌒

The captain of the *Mountaineer* reached into his pocket for a flask and held it up to his ginger-bearded face, wiping his mouth with the back of his hand. Jansen then spat, his pale, red-rimmed eyes looking out to sea.

'We lost her at Thistle Cove. Anchors dragged and she ran aground on the beach.'

He turned back to Anderson and sighed.

'We got off a couple of barrels, brandy and flour, then she broke up.'

Anderson's eyes were fixed on his face and Jansen looked away.

'You'd have a good camp here, wouldn't you?'

His eyes ran across the top of the sandhills and to the thicket of trees that lay behind them. Manning followed his gaze. Anderson's hut was completely hidden from view. Jansen focused again on Anderson and the thumb that stroked the barrel of the musket.

'We're just waitin' for the wind to change. And ... well ... there are women.'

'The wind has changed,' said Anderson.

But all the same he looked at the women who stood clutching each other a short distance away, their bonnets screening their faces until the taller one looked up and met his gaze briefly. He turned back to Jansen and inclined his head towards the boat.

'Well I ain't feeding you for nothing so you better find a way to pay me.'

Manning watched the men empty the boat. The one who was familiar caught his eye. Manning saw him untie the sail and fold it. He stepped back and walked around to the other side of the boat, letting someone else lift the sail higher up the beach. Manning thought he knew then who it was. The man he was thinking of was slightly built and had reminded him of a ship's rat because of his sharp face and small, dark, shifty eyes. The man reached down and threw something that landed at the edge of the granite where the contents of the boat had been unloaded. The other men lifted the whaleboat onto wooden rollers and brought it into the corner of the bay well above the high-tide mark. Manning realised he had been staring for some time and hoped that no one had noticed. He put his hands in his trousers where there had once been pockets and walked slowly up over the granite, trying to convince himself that it couldn't be the same person. The man with a face like a rat turned and watched Manning disappear over the headland.

When Manning reached the other side of the rock the work had almost been done. The women had boiled the soft white fat into clear oil. Some skins had been rubbed with salt and others would be dried. The men sat in a half-circle on rocks that poked out of the sand, cleaning their knives while the boy Jimmy took a bucket of water to the whaleboat and washed out the blood. Seeing Manning, they stopped what they were doing, curious to know who was visiting their island.

'Twas Jansen,' said Manning to Isaac, who asked.

Isaac tugged at his long thick beard, straightening it. He looked over towards his woman. She was called Mooney because she had a round face. Manning could see her climbing over the rocks looking for shellfish. But her face wasn't round any more and he knew that the clear whites of her eyes were now tinged with yellow.

Manning had been with Isaac and three sealers from another boat when they took Mooney from the mainland near Kangaroo Island. Manning was told to keep his mouth shut while they waited in the bush. They grabbed Mooney as she passed and another woman who fought like a polecat. He felt for his ear where Isaac had cuffed him for letting her get away. Mooney had squirmed like a dying snake and the baby at her breast was torn from her and left in the dirt, screaming. Three men held her as they pulled and dragged her towards the boat. She wailed in a way that made Manning think she would summon a strange spirit to crack open the red earth. He had hurried to get into the boat. She sat at the stern facing him. Her head slumped forward. And as he pulled on the oar, blood from her nose dripped onto the wooden deck and into the water lying at the bottom where it swirled like thin red ribbon. He pulled again on the oar and peered over the top of her head at the line of breakers, which surged towards the shore. A dark figure entered the water. When he didn't come up Isaac and the others laughed. A couple of days later they said they were going to hunt kangaroo. Afterwards, he heard how they went back and took two men around the point and shot them and beat out their brains with clubs.

Manning didn't like Isaac very much, especially when he was in one of his moods. His eyes seemed to widen then and bulge, and the black bit in the middle stood out so that it looked as though he had fish eyes. They all kept out of his way. Usually he went after Mooney and bashed her. One time though he hit Sal by mistake and that's how he came to have a red knife mark along his cheek. For Anderson didn't like other men messing with his women.

'Baccy Isaac?'

'Son of a bitch,' said Isaac in the same way he always did.

Manning stood scratching his lank sandy hair for a moment. Isaac had never parted with any of his tobacco before but it never stopped Manning from asking. When he turned away he stubbed his toe on a rock. He swore under his breath. The boy Jimmy giggled. Manning swung around as though to clip him for laughing at him.

But instead he spat: 'Little bastard.'

Isaac's eyes narrowed and he said to no one in particular: 'So … Jansen's back.'

⁓

At the place where two rocks sat like stone tablets, leaning against each other, Manning met the young lad from Jansen's boat coming the other way. He had brown eyes, a protruding bottom lip that made him look a bit simple, and a thick lock of brown hair which flopped across his forehead. He seemed to be wandering aimlessly. But when he saw Manning he took his hands out of his coat pockets and grinned.

'James Newell. Jem, most people know me as.'

Manning nodded. 'Got any bacca?'

The lad pulled out a small bundle wrapped in oilskin from his pocket. 'Yeah, I nicked it, when they was unloading the boat.'

Manning hadn't expected him to have any. It was just something to say. But he took it and they walked on until they reached the water's edge and sat down.

'Where are you from?' he asked as his mouth flooded with saliva and diluted the bitterness. He looked sideways at the boy, eyes half closed. He thought they were about the same age, maybe the lad was a bit younger. He gave him back the rest of the tobacco.

'Surrey in England. Came out on the *James Pattison* last year. To King George Sound. Me dad's a labourer.'

Manning grunted and spat.

'What you doing with Jansen?'

The boy stared ahead at some point on the horizon.

'Work. Van Diemen's Land.'

'What? There ain't nothing at the Sound?'

Jem shook his head slowly and his hair fell over his forehead. He flicked it back.

'Me dad … we done a bit of thatching and that. But it ain't enough to feed us.'

'I heard they was paying good money in the west.'

'When there's work,' said Jem. 'But it ain't often and people stopped coming. Me dad he was mad when we got here. It ain't how it's supposed to be.'

Small waves rolled over the point, swirled onto the sand in front of them and then retreated, leaving behind little bracelets of foam. Manning spat a lump of tobacco-stained phlegm onto the rock where it lay glistening. He wondered what they had expected.

'What about the women?'

'They're me sisters.'

Manning turned to him and pursed his lips. They were black at the corners.

'They taken?'

'Jansen's got one of them.'

'And the other one?'

'She's married.'

January 1886

I want to speak to you. To tell you what happened after you left. I had a daughter. Called Mary, after you. I heard you died somewhere in Sydney. I had lost you before then though. I wish we could go back to the island. We didn't know that it would change everything. Since then the years have stretched thinly like a rubber band pulled tight. The days are shorter and harder. I want to spring back to the beginning.

I am alone. Except for George. He is my fourth husband. He never comes into my room. He listens on the landing. There is no one left. Our sisters, Henrietta and Caroline, married and left with their husbands. I have not heard of them for many years now. And our parents and our brothers are dead.

Do you remember the day we sailed? When I close my eyes I hear the swell of the sea slapping the side of the boat as the breeze pushes us along. I see too the long dark tentacles of cloud stretching across the sky and smothering our sun.

Middle Island 1835, Dorothea Newell

Dorothea knew it would be safer on the mainland than on some island in the middle of nowhere. Not that it made any difference. She and her sister Mary would have to do what everyone else did.

She saw how every time the swell rolled around the point and broke over the wreck of the *Mountaineer*, the sea claimed a little more of the damaged vessel. She felt heavy with dread at the thought of leaving the narrow beach, defined by smooth, steep rock on either side, in a small whaleboat. The natives had been friendly, showing them the freshwater lake behind the sandhill and how to dig for the root of an edible reed. But Captain Jansen wanted to leave. He said there were too many of them for the whaleboat to make it to the Sound. They would leave for an island where there was a sealer's camp. It was to the east not far from the coast. Jansen said the sealer had a large whaleboat and supplies and he could help them return to the Sound. Dorothea watched his mouth open and close as he spoke. She felt like a wooden doll that was being worked by an unseen hand. Her sister too was stultified by fear. They watched the men load the whaleboat with casks of water and what was left of the hard biscuit. The kegs of flour and brandy that had been taken from the wreck before the tide came in were placed in the middle and slightly to the front of the boat for balance. Two men went back up the beach for the sail, which had been their shelter in the corner of the bay. She and her sister were told to get in. They helped each other. The sail was pulled up the mast and they rowed past the steep headland and out into the open sea where the canvas caught the wind.

⌒

The boat slid into the deep troughs of the swell. It was like being in a valley of the sea where at the bottom there was no horizon. Dorothea's stomach felt as though it was full of foam. She wondered if the whaleboat would come up the other side before a wave curled over the stern and pulled them in. After a while she closed her eyes, feeling the moisture seep into her skin. If the sea chose to take her, would she die from the cold or would she have to drown? The boat came up the other side and her eyes opened and fixed on a rock somewhere along that hazy line that separated the sea from the sky. She realised that in three days of sailing she had barely moved except when they hauled up on the beach at night. The rock loomed larger. It was in the middle of a strip of grey land. There was a white beach to one side. The whiteness was bright after so much blue and grey.

⌒

Dorothea took the rough hand of the young man without looking at him. She held her skirts above her ankles and clambered over the side onto hard sand. Her fingers were stiff from clutching the rough timber of the boat and it was an effort to straighten her legs. She tried to moisten her lips with her tongue but it stuck to her teeth. Her sister stumbled as she was helped from the boat. Dorothea took her arm to help her and to steady herself. They both shivered as they walked a little way up the beach. Mary started to weep hot tears that drew lines down the salty veneer of her face. She glanced over her shoulder at the black man by the boat. His stare was steady, his eyes blank but hard beneath his heavy brow. She looked to the younger man and saw the sickly smile in his eyes as they shifted with excitement from her to her sister. She had never seen anything like them before: the big man with his shiny black skull and broad frame draped in animal skins, and the young one, lank hair falling to his shoulders and strips of trousers flapping around his ankles. Her eyes watered and she looked away, blinking against the shimmering figures that moved across the sand. She squeezed her sister's hand but her grip had lost its strength.

Mary began to breathe quickly.

'I need something to drink.'

Dorothea released her. She looked into her sister's face seeing the sweat on her forehead even though they faced the wind. Exhaustion was smudged beneath her eyes. The black man had his back to them, talking to Jansen. When she approached, Jansen draped his arm across her shoulders.

'My love,' he sniggered.

'Is there any water? My sister is poorly.' Her voice was flat.

She could feel the sealer's dark eyes upon her. He smelt like a fox.

'Follow the edge of the rock. There's a well at the back.'

He pointed to the corner of the beach where the sandhill sloped into a low ridge towards the granite. A clump of wattle grew there and behind it was stubby bush, coloured red and gold and green.

Although they couldn't see the camp from the beach, they could make out a track around the wattle where thin gold leaves blanketed the ground. They followed his directions, keeping to the edge of the granite as it went inland. The bush was on their left and grey-black lumpy rock striped with shallow gullies on their right. Their feet trampled dried-up plants that hadn't survived the summer and dry yellow lichen which clung tenaciously to life at the base of the granite. Just when they were beginning to think the track led nowhere, they glimpsed something through the trees and caught the familiar smell of a smouldering hearth. A gap in the wattle turned into a path to a large timber and stone hut, which was built on the edge of a thicket of tall paperbark trees. They came to a wall and followed it around to the other side where they were surprised to discover that attached to the building was a shelter like a verandah which opened out into the clearing. Bedrolls and piles of skins were kept underneath it. A door at one end led to a kitchen. At the other end was an entrance to a storeroom that contained barrels and skins. From the rafters hung dead animals: wallabies, geese and a large lizard. A big paperbark tree and a tall eucalypt with a straight smooth trunk sheltered the clearing. Beyond both trees the ground sloped sharply upwards. It was the sandhill that hid the hut from the eyes of anyone on the beach. It was a well-built hut, better than their house at the Sound. And it was so sheltered. Not a whisper of wind stirred below, although the tops of the trees shook now and then with the occasional gust.

They remembered the sealer had said the well was around the back. From where they had been standing on the beach, he must have meant the side of the hut that faced inland. So they walked around the hut, alongside the kitchen wall and then to the stone fireplace and chimney that jutted out from the corner of the south-facing wall and into the paperbark thicket. A path of hardened black sand wove in and out of the pale trunks of the trees and through them they glimpsed the ring of granite rocks at the end of it. They lifted the wooden cover. Leaves of the canopy above were reflected in the well's still depths.

The water was soft and icy in their cupped hands. So sweet, it trickled down the sides of their mouths and wetted the fronts of their gowns. Mary splashed her face and tried to rub the salt from her skin. A rush of wind rustled the leaves above. There was a muffled booming sound of distant surf crashing on rock, and the haunting, echoing call of a bronze-wing pigeon. Dorothea undid her bonnet and her shawl. Her clothes felt oily and damp. She took the pail from her sister and filled it as full as she had the strength to carry, then tipped it over her head. Gasping, she grinned at Mary through a dripping veil, her thick brown hair loosened and falling about her face. She handed her sister the pail.

'Tis cold,' said Mary but took it anyway.

Although their features were similar, Mary was slighter in build and her hair was dark. They were both thin, their skin drawn tightly across their cheekbones. When they were soaked, Dorothea noticed a track leading through the trees and followed it into the sunlight. The track led them to the granite rock without going back to the hut. It took them further south past another small clearing to their left where there was a dome-shaped dwelling and the charred remains of a small fire. There was also a small garden enclosed by a brush fence. Sheltered from view, they lay down to rest. The heat of the rock radiated through their skin and into their chilled aching bones. They gave in to it. Soon the silence was broken only by their gentle breathing, the scurrying of little lizards through the debris at the base of the rock, and the insistent but intermittent buzz of an insect.

'Dorothea.'

As the sound left Mary's mouth it seemed to linger in the air for a moment.

'Mmm.'

'What are we going to do?'

Mary rolled onto her side and looked at her sister who lay on her back, eyes closed to the sun.

'Don't know.'

'How are we going to get back?'

'Don't know.' Dorothea sighed and sat up, blinking as her eyes adjusted to the brightness of the afternoon light.

'He's not going to take us.'

'Who?' asked Dorothea.

'The sealer.'

Dorothea shrugged and said: 'Perhaps there'll be a trader.'

'That could be months.'

'There'll be ships that pass here.'

'Do you think so?'

Dorothea paused and took a deep breath in an attempt to stave off a sick feeling at the bottom of her stomach. 'We'll get back to the Sound,' she said.

'In that boat?'

'Look, the thing is we're here. We didn't drown. We have each other. Jem's with us and you have Matthew.'

'He's a savage.'

'Who? Your husband?' She smiled briefly.

'No, that man, the sealer.'

'They're all savages,' muttered Dorothea.

Mary sighed and looked down at the rock, flicking the pale green lichen with her fingernail.

'Matthew's alright. At least he doesn't hit me.'

A pigeon burst noisily from the undergrowth. They both jumped.

Dorothea watched her sister as she lowered her head onto her knees and she remembered the night Matthew had come to their house at the Sound. He called out from the doorway that he had bread and cheese and grog. From her place by the fire she had wondered what the occasion was. She came into the room for entertaining, pushing aside the piece of canvas that hung in the doorway. Mother was sitting unsteadily on her stool, as she seemed to do more often, scattering snuff over her knees. Matthew was standing inside the door, jiggling the coins in his pocket. He said he had money for a gown. Father took the bottle from him and broke the bread and cheese. He filled two glasses with glowing amber and they swallowed together. She fetched Mary and Henrietta and they stood with their backs against the wall. He would choose Mary.

There was no money in the new colony but that didn't stop Matthew from wanting to sever his ties with the man who had brought him from England. All of sudden he noticed other indentured servants abandoning their masters for land of their own. Although he couldn't afford it, he wanted to be able to say that he was no longer a servant of the Resident Magistrate's household. Jem, his new brother-in-law, told him the stories that he had heard down at the harbour. Of where there was money to be found. When the captain of the *Mountaineer* sailed into the harbour offering for just three pounds a passage to the east, Matthew was easily persuaded. While they were preparing to sail, Dorothea decided to go with them. She hadn't wanted her sister to leave and neither had she found work after her mistress's husband died of consumption. And Captain Jansen had offered her a free passage. He had also promised to buy her a gown.

⌒

Dorothea looked up and watched tufts of cloud arch over the endless blue. One passed over the sun and suddenly it was cool. They gathered up their shawls and put on their bonnets. As they retraced their steps Dorothea, who was walking ahead, untied her bonnet again. Mary caught up with her.

'What are you doing?'

'I don't want it.'

The ties were crisp with salt and had rubbed a sore under her chin. She threw it into the bush.

'But you can't.'

Dorothea came around the side of the hut and almost walked into the man who had directed them from the beach. Mary bumped into the back of her. Dorothea wished now that she had kept her bonnet. At eye level was silver fur and hard black skin. She looked up. He had a purple scar under his eye.

'You found the well?' His voice sounded in his chest.

Dorothea nodded.

'Get some water for tea.'

The sealer turned away. She stood there for a moment clasping her hands, squeezing them until they hurt and then letting go. Mary nudged her. They peered through the doorway into the kitchen. The room was full of eye-watering smoke. A long trestle table stood in the middle. Along each side of it was rough wooden seating. The air was heavy with a strong rancid smell that reminded Dorothea of the stench of dull-eyed fish at the end of market day. The floor was paved with lumps of granite that had been dug into the black dirt. There was a doorway into another room. But they didn't go through it. Dorothea reached for the poker that hung at the side of the fireplace and stoked up the fire while Mary went to fetch the water. She looked over her shoulder, half expecting him to be standing behind her, but he must have gone through the other doorway which was shielded by a piece of canvas.

⁓

Just before the sun disappeared, golden light edged the scrub at the top of the sandhill and softened the men's harsh features. Some of them sat on tree stumps and logs, while others sprawled or squatted in the dirt in front of the verandah. A small fire spat and crackled in the middle of the clearing. Occasionally one of them would lean over towards it and take out a stick to light a pipe. Flasks of drink were shared and the sound of their voices rose and fell like the waves, which could be heard, more loudly now, crashing on the beach.

Dorothea and Mary watched the Aboriginal women tend to a pot over the fire. Although the air was dense inside the hut, they preferred it to the atmosphere outside and the voracious stares of the men. One of the black women added dark bloody meat and a vegetable that looked like a yam. The other two chopped and sliced at the other end of the table, their breasts swaying against their dusty bellies.

Dorothea found their nakedness disturbing. She thought that they should wear clothes like the natives at the Sound. It made them less like savages. She remembered the day the black women were given their red flannel dresses. She had been on the shore with Mary, looking longingly at the clothes worn by the women who had just arrived from England, when a wooden crate was lifted off the pilot boat. It was hacked open there on the landing and they could see it was full of red fabric. They were told it had been sent by a group of English society ladies and a duchess to protect the modesty of the natives. Later that day the black women were rounded up and brought down to the harbour. They came in small groups, some shrieking with laughter and others giggling shyly as they held up the dresses and inspected them closely. A few put them on. The magistrate told them that they had to wear them if they wanted to come into the settlement for tea or flour or sugar. When the women left, Dorothea remembered thinking how strange it was to see flashes of red between the trees as they slipped back into the bush.

Occasionally the two women at the end of the table looked up but just as quickly they turned away again. Dorothea tried to catch their eyes. After a while she looked at Mary.

'Are you hungry?'

'I think so.'

The last time they had eaten was in the whaleboat. They had shared bits of mouldy biscuit between nine of them. Now there was just a knot where Dorothea's stomach was. But the juicy smell of meat stewing caused her mouth to moisten and the knot to unravel.

She mused, half to herself: 'What is it, do you think?'

The sealer entered and glanced over.

'Tammar stew.' It was hard to read his expression. 'I taught them to make it. They use the wallaby on the island. They call them tammar.'

Dorothea looked at Mary and then back at him and asked: 'What are their names?'

He stared at her and she wished she hadn't spoken.

'Who?'

'Their names.' She nodded towards the fire. 'The women,' she added almost under her breath.

He walked over to the tallest of the three and grasped her short matted hair. He turned her to face them.

'Dinah. Say hello to the fine English ladies.' His tone was sarcastic.

She glanced up briefly and mumbled something.

'She can speak like you if she wants to.' He gestured with his other arm. 'This one's Sal and that's Mooney.'

Sal giggled, revealing a wide white grin. Mooney looked at the floor. Dinah continued to stare ahead at some point on the wall behind them. At that moment Matthew, Mary's husband, appeared at the doorway. He looked around and then went to stand behind Mary. He placed his hand at the nape of her neck, his eyes on the other man. Mary looked down at her hands, which were clasped tightly on the table. No one moved.

Dorothea watched an ant as it crawled along the edge of the table. Matthew straightened.

'I'll be outside,' he said.

⁓

The light in the room had dimmed. The sealer appeared as a shape in the other doorway. He had put on a shirt with sleeves torn from the shoulders. It hung over the animal skin wrapped around his hips. He reached for a lamp that was hanging from a hook on the wall. He placed it in the middle of the table and filled it with oil. Lit, it illuminated his broad forehead, shadowing his eyes and deepening the lines that ran down the side of his nose to his mouth. He had shaved with his sealing knife, leaving behind a few shiny dots of congealed blood on his neck and at the back of his skull.

⁓

The black women left and they ate their meal undisturbed. Pushing her plate away, Dorothea reached across the table for her sister's hand. Her eyes glittered in the light of the lamp as she looked back at Dorothea.

'How do you feel?'

Mary shrugged in a way that suggested even that was an effort.

'Jem said there is a tent in the trees near the beach.'

They stood in the shadow of the verandah, looking out to the clearing. Three men sat against the trunk of the eucalypt, legs stretched out in front of them. Some were lying in the dirt having unrolled their bedding. The sealer was talking to a man they hadn't seen before. His beard was long and thick, an animal-skin cloak around his shoulders. He was sitting with legs bent, arms resting on his knees. One hand clasped a clay pipe, which he used now and then to stab the air. He used the other hand to tug at his beard. They were both talking in low voices, heads close together. The man with the beard glanced over at Jansen and stood up. He walked to the edge of the clearing where another small fire burnt healthily. The Aboriginal women were squatted before it. Mooney poked a stick into the coals. The man leant down and took her arm. He pulled her upright and led her towards a bundle of skins beside the wall.

Their brother left the fire and walked towards them.

'Jem,' Dorothea called out softly. 'Jem.'

'Bleedin' Jesus, Sis, you give us a fright.'

'Can you take us to the tent?'

'It's through there.'

'Please Jem.'

They disappeared quietly through the trees. Dorothea looked back. The thin pale trunks of the paperbark trees glowed in the moonlight. They half circled the camp and looked like silver bars. She hurried to keep up. Through a gap in the bush she could see the beach. The wind had dropped and the silky sea unfolded towards the mainland where a path was lit by the moon. Near the island it rippled silver and dispersed into flashing bits of light that caught the top of the waves as they swelled and tumbled onto the sand.

Jem said something to Mary that Dorothea couldn't hear.

'I said I'm going out tomorrow with Anderson.'

'With who?'

'The sealer.'

'What for?'

'Sealing, what do you think?'

'Are they all going?'

'Don't know … that James Manning told him I wanted to work. He says he'll pay me when he takes a load to the Sound.'

Jem left them in front of the tent. It had been erected beneath wattle trees that were bent over by the wind. From the entrance they could see the edge of the rock that led out towards the headland and to the beach. She could see that they would be sheltered from most weather and they were fortunate tonight for it was warm. Wattle leaves covered their floor and smelt musty. They would sweep them out tomorrow but for now they used the loose canvas from one side for a mat. Taking off their shoes they lay down, covering their bodies with their shawls and lying close together for comfort.

Dorothea woke with the hand of her sister grabbing her arm tightly. It was night and there were voices. Drunken voices of men. She recognised Matthew's voice.

'She's my wife.'

There was scuffling and branches were broken. Someone fell heavily and grunted.

'There ... now get off.'

Matthew crawled on his hands and knees into the tent, breathing heavily. The air saturated with the cloying smell of alcohol. His hand grabbed Mary's thigh. He leant on it and pushed himself up. She gasped and wriggled to shift the pressure.

'Mary,' he said hoarsely.

He reached over her stomach to the other side of her waist and pulled her towards him. There was no resistance and he lay heavily across her, grunting as he did so. He fumbled about with her skirts, tugging them up under his legs, and opened his trousers. Mary made a small sound. His breathing quickened.

Someone was outside. Dorothea's breath caught at the back of her throat. Matthew froze and then knelt between his wife's legs. He leapt up and crashed through the entrance of the tent and then there was a slapping sound, the sound of skin on skin and silence. Matthew returned and lay beside his wife. Mary let go of her sister's arm. Dorothea had been comfortable before but now she noticed that underneath her right shoulder there was a lump in the ground and a place in the small of her back ached. She turned on her side, away from her sister, and listened to the shoosh of the waves.

January 1886

George has not come into my bedroom for days. He is waiting for me to die. I can hear it in his footsteps that tread the wide wooden stairs. I want to call out but my mouth is too dry. From my bed, which lies in the corner of the room, I see the violet twilight framed in the small squares of the window.

I remember when you married Matthew at the magistrate's Strawberry Hill Farm. How pretty you looked in the light linen gown he had bought you. The sun was high in the sky and the bush was loud with the sound of insects.

Middle Island 1835, James Manning

A man left the hut and walked towards them. Manning and Jem were on the edge of the clearing, their backs against the paperbark thicket, with a view of the others. The man sat on a tree stump close by. His features were indistinguishable in the twilight but Manning decided that he looked as though he was in his twenties. He had dark hair and eyes set close together. Jem told Manning that his name was Matthew and that he was his sister's husband.

Anderson moved like a shadow out of the house and around the back.

'Who is he?' asked Matthew.

'Black Jack Anderson,' replied Manning. 'You ain't heard of him?'

Matthew and Jem shook their heads.

'Came from Kangaroo Island. Deserter they reckon from a Yankee whaler.'

Manning paused and looked at one then the other.

'No one knows anything about him. It's how he wants it. They reckon he's been around these parts before. There was a fellow who worked for him once ...'

Manning's feet were getting cramp and he stretched them out in front of him.

'What happened?' asked Jem.

'He cut him ear to ear. They say he's under a waterfall at Doubtful Island Bay near the Sound. The water washing over him keeps him from going rotten.' Manning narrowed his eyes for effect.

Matthew stared thoughtfully ahead, picking at the skin on his lip.

'There was another fellow called Anderson who was a sealer, last year in the pub at the Sound. He was from Kangaroo Island. But he was white.'

Manning raised his eyebrows but he was no longer interested in what was being said for the food was coming out. Dinah and Mooney brought out the pot and placed it on the table under the porch. Manning watched but he didn't get up. Experience had taught him to wait. Men pushed themselves up off the dirt and milled around. The sound of the spoon clattering on tin plates interrupted their words. By the time it was Manning's turn there was just a layer left at the bottom.

There was only Jem who hadn't eaten. He spooned most of it onto his plate and took a piece of bread, returning to his position in the shadows. Jem followed, stepping over the fellow Manning had noticed earlier, the one who looked like a rat.

'Do you know him?' asked Manning.

Jem shrugged. 'I think his name is Owens.'

Manning sat down. He shook his head slightly in disbelief. But he had known all along that what he suspected was true. He turned to Jem, barely able to speak.

'What's he doing on the *Mountaineer*?' he stuttered.

'Don't know.'

Jem looked at him strangely.

Manning rubbed his sparse beard with his forefinger. He swallowed the meat that suddenly seemed foul in his mouth.

'Who are the others?' he asked more clearly.

Jem had finished the small amount on his plate and looked over at Manning's plate and the others who were still eating.

'Don't know,' he shrugged. 'Him over there … I know him. He's the swell they call William Church.'

Firelight flickered over a man in a dark suit and a hat, a plate balanced on his knees. Manning picked up the bone which was buried in sticky gravy and placed it between his teeth, sucking the marrow and watching Jem from the corner of his eyes. He knew that Jem was trying not to look at the food on his plate. Matthew left to relieve himself in the bush.

'You can have it for the baccy.'

'What?'

'Me plate.' Manning had eaten about half the contents of it.

'That ain't no deal.'

Manning brought his knife up to his mouth.

'I'm not givin' it away. If Jansen knew,' said Jem, looking over his shoulder.

Manning shrugged and then said quietly. 'Please yourself but I can look after you.'

'How?'

'You know what I mean.'

He nodded at the men who surrounded them. One of them was cleaning his knife. Manning carefully poked his teeth with a twig. He spat in the dirt. Jem put his hand in his pocket and handed Manning the rest of the tobacco.

Manning saw Jem's brother-in-law return from the bush and into the firelight, buttoning his trousers and carefully stepping between the huddles of men. But in the half-light he stood on a plate that belonged to one of Anderson's men. Manning knew what was coming and he was glad it wasn't him. Johno leapt up as though on a spring and pushed Matthew so that he stumbled. Matthew recovered his balance and swung around into the glinting blade of a knife.

'Hey Johno. Twas an accident.'

Mead, another of Anderson's men, stood up between them. His cheeks glowed in the light as he turned towards Matthew.

'He's real touchy. Anderson found him on a rock. He'd been living on penguins for a year. Could've been longer. He can't remember. Some sealer was supposed to come back for him. Never did, did they Johno?'

Matthew glanced sideways at Johno who still held his knife out in front of him. Johno's arm dropped and he bent down and picked up his plate and returned to his place in the dirt.

'Francis Mead,' said the man, facing Matthew.

'Matthew Gill.'

They nodded at each other.

Manning looked over at Johno who silently shovelled sandy food with his knife. His cold furious eyes darted about like a gull's. Manning moved along the log so that Matthew could sit down. He could see that he was shaken.

'Fellows are always like that,' said Manning. 'Except for Mead. He's alright as long as you don't give him a reason.'

The fire had dwindled to a few coals. Men snored and talked softly. Manning spat the remains of his tobacco. He squatted, looking into the fading light, and then straightened and headed into the bush. Small animals rustled the undergrowth. He turned and buttoned himself up. A twig snapped. He stood still and felt for his knife. A pulse boomed in his ear and his breath came hard and fast.

A voice to the side hissed: 'So 'tis James Manning.'

Manning turned slowly towards it.

'Owens.'

Even though the man's face was in shadow, Manning recognised the sharp-nosed profile.

'So you know me.'

'Couldn't forget.'

Owens chuckled without humour. Manning wondered how he came to be in the West. They had both been on the *Defiance*. When it was wrecked off New South Wales, Owens had gone in the longboat back to Sydney. Briefly Manning wondered what had happened to the others, but he didn't care so he didn't ask. He turned to leave.

'Where are you going?'

Manning stopped and looked back. He couldn't see Owens's little eyes but he knew they were on him.

'I was enjoying our little get-together.'

Moonlight caught a glint of his tooth. The rest of his face was partly obscured by the spidery shadows of branches. Manning tried to control the shudder that gripped his shoulders. He trod heavily on the path back to the clearing.

He stared without focusing at the embers, wrestling with a green stick until it snapped in half. The crack brought him back and he threw the two pieces into the fire. He looked up as Jem reappeared from the darkness. Manning unrolled his bedding and gave Jem one of his kangaroo skins since the night was warm enough without it.

Grey, early morning light. Treetops, dark shapes against an insipid sky. Manning rolled over onto his stomach and lifted his head, resting his chin on his palm. Bodies covered in furs were like giant caterpillars stretched out under the verandah and across the clearing. Standing over one of them was Isaac. Slowly Manning lowered his head so that his chin was resting on the ground. He didn't like the fact that Isaac had a knife in his hand.

Isaac kicked the body beneath him. He kicked again, bringing his foot up higher. A head lifted slowly. Manning realised it was Jansen. He seemed unable to speak. The captain of the *Mountaineer* hauled himself up, one side of his face pockmarked with the imprint of sticks and seeds. He was shaking. Manning wondered if Isaac would cut him.

'We want your whaleboat.'

Jansen nodded like a cork bobbing in the swell. Manning could see that Isaac was grinning. Although he wasn't tall like Anderson, he looked big because there was so much hair on his head and face. Manning thought that Isaac looked like the keeper of Davy Jones's Locker.

'You be needing men. To take oars,' spluttered Jansen.

Manning could see that Jansen thought he was dead. That Isaac was going to kill him for his whaleboat.

But Isaac just nodded and said with a savage grin: 'Aye, we'll be needing you and your men.'

He waved the blade across the bundles of men. Manning could see they weren't asleep either. Just lying low like he was. Then he noticed Anderson leaning against a timber post that held up the verandah. He had been watching.

'That's enough. Get these men up.'

He turned his back and disappeared into the hut. Isaac continued to stand over Jansen with the knife pointed at his neck but he looked around.

'Get down to the beach ... all of you. If you want to eat that is. You too.'

He pressed the tip of the knife against Jansen's skin, chuckling.

'That'll teach you. Thinking you could haul up here and eat your way through our supplies. We work for our food.'

Then he withdrew and followed Anderson into the hut. Manning heard Jem let out his breath. He hadn't noticed he was awake. They got up with everyone else and stowed their bedding under the shelter. The black women passed through the clearing on their way to the beach. They were naked except for amulets of shells and bone around their necks.

The beach looked bleak in the cold light. Pale cloud arched overhead. There was a strip of yellow and brown cloud over the mainland where there had been a fire. The breeze, although light, seemed to have moved into the northwest. Their footsteps squeaked on the sand and before them an oily sea rippled, colourless except for the occasional white flash of foam marking the place where the swell broke over a rock. A black and white gull circled. Its mate appeared and they both glided and flapped overhead, calling to one another: Caw, caw.

Manning noticed William Church walking beside him. He was tying his stock in the way that people who wear stocks do. He reached into the top pocket of his coat for a piece of cloth and wiped his face. When he put it back, it fell out. He bent down to pick it up but a fellow who Manning recognised as one of the crew from the *Mountaineer* thrust his pelvis into his arse and knocked him off balance. He fell on his hands and knees. Manning laughed. Serve the toffy bugger right. Church stood up and wiped the sand from his hands. Jem looked at Manning and grinned. The crewman began to circle Church with one hand on the top of his knife. Manning turned away. Then the fellow saw Anderson watching him and he stopped, but not before he had hissed something under his breath to Church.

⁓

The *Mountaineer's* whaleboat had been lifted to the water's edge. Men surrounded it, looking up at Anderson who stood on the sloping rock. He told them what he wanted and then looked over at Church and asked if he had pulled an oar before. Church shook his head, clasping his pale hands in front of his frockcoat which hung loosely from his thin frame. He told him to get firewood.

Manning and Jem followed Anderson over the headland and heard the men from the *Mountaineer* cursing Anderson. But not loud enough for him to hear. Manning thought they could curse all they like. There wouldn't be anyone who would challenge Anderson. Not when he wore a brace of pistols on his belt. And Manning knew that it wasn't the first time that Anderson had forced men at gunpoint to kill seals for him.

The boy Jimmy skipped ahead, jumping from one boulder to the next. Red-brown skinny legs darted in and out of Manning's vision. He reached the whaleboat before them and stood at the bow, holding onto it and jumping up and down on the spot. They used wooden rollers to take it to the sea. The boat sat lightly in the shallows and they jumped in. But as the boy hooked his leg over, Anderson told him to get off and find some muttonbirds.

Manning took his place at a thwart. Jem had the next oar. They waited for a break in the waves and then moved out into the channel. He watched the boy stare after the boat, little waves lapping around his ankles. He looked over his shoulder at Dinah who sat straight at the bow. Her tightly cropped head held proud and her sad, scarred breasts facing the open sea like a ship's figurehead. Anderson stood over them, guiding them with the steering oar through the shallow channel. They raised the sail and cut diagonally across towards Isaac and the others who had just rounded the point in the *Mountaineer*'s whaleboat. They worked the lee oars to keep the boat close to the wind.

Manning was conscious of his feet resting on thin wooden board. It was all that lay between him and the dark depths of the sea. He hoped the wind wasn't going to get any stronger. Jem's eyes were fixed on the back of the man in front of him. Lean forward, pull back, he looked down the line of the oar as it neatly cut the surface. Waves from the bow fanning out into bruise-coloured water. Sometimes the sun pierced the liquid glass and lit the silver fish and the black shapes that moved between the weed. But today the sea was not throwing up any of its secrets. Manning glanced uneasily up at Anderson.

Behind him the glow on the horizon grew stronger as the sun presented itself through a veil of cloud.

~

They rounded Flinders Peak. The troughs between the waves deepened. Thick banks of water rose and wavered, the little boat rising with them, climbing on an angle and sliding down the other side. They moved in a westerly direction towards an island about a mile ahead. Spray salted their faces and burnt their eyes. Water slapped at the side and ran over into the bottom of the boat where it swirled around their ankles. Soon the rocky island reared up out of the water. Surf surged over its eastern edge and then receded, revealing a black, moss-like weed more treacherous than ice, and dirty white barnacles. Boulders sat at odd angles on the rock just above the waterline, almost indistinguishable from the seals that lay amongst them.

Manning felt his stomach surge with the swell. They reached the calm water in the lee of the island where they lowered the sail and took in the oars. Two gulls had followed. The boat moved gently up and down. The birds circled. The familiar smell of the seal colony reached them, sharp and sickly. And every now and then the wind carried their sounds. Anderson ordered Manning to change positions with the man in front of him. He let go a stone anchor over the side and then waited for a lull in the swell. Dinah was standing, poised at the bow, holding the side with one hand, a club in the other. Mead and Manning were behind her. The sea flattened.

Anderson gave the order to pull while he let out slack on the anchor line. The boat thrust forwards. Jem looked around at Manning. Anderson told him to stay with the oar. Manning knew it was a matter of timing. His heart beat hard against his chest as they surfed in on the swell. Together they must leap from the boat onto the foam-covered ledge. They must reach down for a crack in the rock so that when the sea sucked back they could brace themselves against it and hold tight. If he lost his footing he would roll into the sea like a skinned seal. There was a dull thud at the keel and he followed Dinah over the side. He bent double and scrambled for a foothold. He found it and gripped tight, watching as Anderson held firm the stern anchor line so the boat wouldn't splinter on the rock. Jem and the other oarsman pulled hard on the stern oars but Jem was not quick enough and the surf pushed them sideways. Just as he thought they were going to go over, they straightened and sliced the top of the next wave before reaching calmer water.

Like the others Manning had worn his sealskin shoes to protect his feet from the sharp-edged barnacles. But he had nothing to protect his hands. Bent over they edged slowly and carefully across the slippery surface. Manning fought the urge to hurry, to get off the wet rock before the big wave hit. Finally they made it above the wet black line. They could look around now. Even though they could hear the seals they couldn't see them for the rock was layered and they were on the lower edge. Boulders rose above them like misshapen building blocks. They would have to climb them to get to the seals. Or as Mead had said they could go back into the water and wade around the edge. Manning shook his head. The less he was in the water the better. And then he remembered his dream.

It was always the same dream: he would twist and turn and when he opened his mouth to scream, bubbles would push out, floating upwards. An arm would cross his face, white and shimmering. Then he would realise it was his own and as he thrashed about the light would change to emerald and in the distance the tail of a seal would ripple through ribbons of weed. It would guide him to land, where on silver sand a dark shape would breathe beside him. He'd reach out for it and discover that it was only skin. And if he looked up there would be Mooney or sometimes it'd be Dinah or Sal gazing down on him.

He envied the way seals moved through the water. Sometimes it seemed they were teasing. Look at me they would say as they twirled and bent over backwards. There were some in the water out past the *Mountaineer's* whaleboat. It was hovering behind the break, waiting for a lull.

He and Mead leant against the rock. Dinah squatted beside them. Dark clouds were forming in the northwest, and rising up to meet them was the brown line of smoke that stretched along the mainland.

Manning noticed the orange nippers of a crab in a crack in the rock. He bent closer and it scuttled sideways and alerted the rest of the clan. They sunk out of sight. The wind brought the roar of surf crashing on the other side of the island. Finally Johno cleared the boat, followed by Mooney and Sal. Hindered by the strong pull of the surf, they struggled to stay upright while the boat retreated beyond the waves.

Usually there were only two or three of them who clubbed. But with the extra men on the oars they would get a good catch today. Having another boat meant that Anderson would double his money. Mead told Dinah and Sal to swim around the edge so that they would come up under the seals. The rest of them would surprise them from the top and herd them towards some rocks which formed a natural corral. Manning followed Mead up over the rocks until they reached a ledge. Manning loosened his grip on the club, stretching his fingers. He looked down.

Silver gulls gathered, circling. Just above the waterline were the cows or klapmatches that had recently given birth and the territorial bulls that were gold and brown like the granite. A bronze-bellied mother lay on her back suckling a pup that sprawled across her flipper like a large black leach. A bull rested with his nose pointed towards her, lying between her and the sea, preventing her escape. They were hair seals. Manning knew their skins weren't as valuable as the fur seals but it made good leather, and the blubber they would boil down for lamp oil.

He watched the two women move carefully like cats over the uneven surface. When each one lifted her leg he saw the dusky pink soles of her feet and realised he had once expected them to be black. What he didn't see were the others, shades of their people who moved between them.

They entered the sea close to where they left the boat, slipping slowly into the water. Their sleek heads bobbing along the surface. A seal surfed with them onto the rock. They pushed their chests off the weed and dragged their bodies behind them, following the seal which walked with an exaggerated gait.

The seals stirred. Some lifted their heads. They pointed their noses to the sky and leant back, sniffing the wind. They were suspicious but their eyesight was poor and the salt water had masked the women's scent. Gradually they stopped fidgeting and settled, resting their chins on the rock, almond eyes open and blinking and then closed. When a seal nearby lifted a flipper to scratch its broad quivering hide, Dinah lifted her arm and scratched her side. If it rolled over onto its back, she rolled onto her back.

Manning was sweating. The sky had darkened and the wind had dropped. The sand patches under the sea glowed strangely green. Bright white water skirted the island. Every now and then a wave came from nowhere. It thickened and swept the rock and was sucked back into the sea. On higher ground were the older pups. Some with mothers, some without. They lay sleeping in twos and threes. A seal opened her eyes and stared directly at him. For a brief moment she looked into him and the waves stilled, but then she raised her head and began to move away.

Below, the women stood up. They hit out in frenzy, shrieking with bloodlust or perhaps it was anger or grief. Seals fell over each other. They met the men on the other side and were driven into the rocky corner. It always surprised Manning how quickly the seals moved. And from a distance they looked like sheep, following one another, galloping and bleating. Trapped. They turned, necks wobbling, teeth bared, spitting and red mouthed and roaring. One hit was often not enough. And he had to be quick. Three came at him at once. He swung wildly, barely able to recover from the last before he brought it down again, and again, and again, conscious only that it had to be hard. Those that escaped lolloped away, rolls of fat moving like jelly as their weight shifted from front flippers to back. Around him lay seals that been felled, grey bodies like stumpy tree trunks, sap leaking from their heads.

Seals that reached the safety of the sea bobbed up, straining back towards the island. Their pups, stranded, many motherless, called desperately. Johno reached into a crevice and pulled one out by its back flippers and threw it high in the air. Manning watched it arch over his head and as it did so its flippers moved and its body twisted and then it hit the rock, bouncing a little.

The men moved between the mounds, skinning them quickly. Some were still alive, blowing bubbles through bloody nostrils. Manning was always faintly uneasy with the pink body that remained. Especially the eyes, which appeared larger and blinked. He didn't look around. The women followed, hacking off flippers and slabs of meat that would be wrapped in canvas and hauled across the water to the boat. Mead picked up the thick coil of rope that at one end was secured to the bow of Anderson's whaleboat. When Mead raised his arm, the men pulled the bundles of skin and blubber through the surf. They had to be quick for soon there would be sharks.

When the foam took on a pinkish hue and the boats were loaded, the sharks began to circle. Anderson steered the boat in. Luckily the swell had dropped off and there was no wind. But the storm was close. And as they moved out into the open sea, using only the oars, thunder rumbled in the distance and spears of light flickered above the mainland.

January 1886

Remember our first summer at the Sound. How we were flattened by the sun and the wind that would gust dryly from the north. How our eyes would itch and the hot air was so hard to breathe. We would bring water up the hill to the hut so we could dampen lengths of canvas to hang in the doorway and the windows. But by the time we finished putting them up, they would be dry again. In the afternoon the trees were still and the birds sat quietly. The bush twitched and rustled with the rasping of cicadas. And then if we were on the other side of the hill, for sometimes we took the trail that wound around and down towards Possession Point, there would be a whisper of a breeze that would touch lightly the beads of water on our foreheads. And the fresh scent of the sea would revive us.

Middle Island 1835, Dorothea Newell

Men's voices on the beach woke her. She crouched before the opening of the tent and watched as their dark shapes launched the whaleboat. She thought for a moment that the *Mountaineer*'s whaleboat was leaving without them. But then she saw Anderson and his men. They were preparing to go sealing. Some of them, including her brother Jem, followed Anderson over the rocks. One of the men was turning back towards the camp, his coat-tails blown from behind by the wind. She recognised him. It was William Church. He had spoken to her briefly on the deck of the *Mountaineer,* saying that he had noticed her small posy of blue flowers pinned above her chest. He told her that it was a rare colour for flowers.

The beach was bare and through the crack in the canvas it looked less forbidding than before. Leaves that were slightly damp stuck to her knees. She pushed her hair off her face and coarse grains on her hands scratched her skin. Behind her, Matthew and her sister slept. He lay on his back, mouth open, black whiskers and hair flecked with sand as though he had a skin disorder. When he was asleep his face softened and he looked as though he might have been kind. The dark spikes of her sister's eyelashes rested in a gentle curve on her pale skin. Her breath was light and even.

Dorothea crawled from the tent, her boots and shawl under one arm. She straightened and felt the moist breeze on her face and noticed the faint smell of smoke. Her head felt heavy and a place behind her eyes ached. She sat down to put on her boots and then decided against it. There didn't seem to be anyone about. She walked through the low scrub to the beach, barefoot and hair loose down her back. When she reached the sand she stood still for a moment, letting it seep between her toes, a thick liquid that caressed and tickled the sensitive arches of her feet.

Her skirts rustled and billowed behind her. She noticed the pause and then the crash as the waves broke on the beach. She decided to walk away from the camp to the other headland, which trailed out into a thin strip into the sea. Just off its point was another low-lying island. For every few steps she took, another wave broke.

～

She had sometimes escaped to the beach at the Sound. Their home was on the hillside facing away from the sea. Surrounding it was bush, dense with robust tall trees that shed their bark. One day she found a thin trail that led to a horseshoe bay where her feet sunk into wet grey sand. She discovered that it was comforting to wander along its shoreline because it was neither suffocating like the bush nor empty like the sea. It was somewhere in between. When she turned around she would step into her footprints and follow them home.

She remembered the day she and her family had arrived. Father leading them from the landing along a dirt track between lumpy lime-washed huts thatched with reeds and people standing in front of their canvas tents tending their fires and staring with an expression she didn't recognise. Later she realised it was smugness for what they already knew.

Before reaching King George Sound they had spent a week in a tent on the beach at Fremantle. There their father had learnt that all the town blocks of the Sound had been taken. So when they arrived he borrowed a horse and a cart from a man called Digby. He led the horse while Mother followed, carrying William on her hip although he was too big for her, the wet hem of her skirt trailing in the dirt. Dorothea and Mary walked behind their mother. The others sat without speaking on the back of the cart, too tired to take the last steps of their long journey. As they climbed higher the bush grew thicker. They left the little cottages and the half-finished huts and tents behind. The smell, which she had first caught on the wind as the line of the coast grew nearer, became stronger.

It was thick like honey. The noise of the bush surrounded the sound of their footsteps as they scuffed the dry dirt. Turning back towards the sea, the horizon unravelled emptily. And the bush to the east and to the west was so much of the same that it hurt her eyes.

～

The wind blew her hair forward on her face. She tucked it behind her ears. Holding it with one hand she knelt down to a clump of seaweed in front of her. A shell the size of her hand shimmered in the sand. Silver ripples that changed to pink and green when held at different angles to the light. She turned it over. On the other side it was coarse and brown. She reached the end of the beach and watched the waves roll over a reef a little way out. Breakers quivered as they came to full height. Briefly they offered a glimpse into another world. Too soon a foamy film came down like a blind and the wave was reduced to a ripple at her feet. Hair whipped her face but she didn't feel it. She breathed deeply and her mind felt clear and whole. She was not afraid any more.

～

The air was heavy in the hollow behind the beach. Flies crawled over plates left in the dirt. Dorothea and Mary gathered them up and the pot with gravy congealed on its sides. The flies swarmed over their heads. They heard the snapping of branches as someone pushed their way through the undergrowth on the other side of the clearing. Both stopped and looked. Dorothea flicked a fly from her face. Bush tops swayed.

'Tis only that man, Church,' she said, relieved, as he emerged from the wattle.

Later she made tea and brought him out a cup. He took it with both hands. She sat on a stump a short distance away. The hem of her gown, which was torn and beginning to fray, was smudged with black dirt. She rested her chin in her hands and stared into the bush. She could feel his eyes on her and she wondered what he saw. A pleasant-faced woman who was slightly soiled, or perhaps he just wondered why she wasn't married. He would think she had nice hair for they all thought that. And her eyes too, they were green like her grandmother's. She was strong with good shoulders and well-shaped arms. But her gown was her mother's and she spoke badly. Eventually he turned away. Her eyes followed his to the raven in the branch above them. Its blue-black feathers glinted as it hopped from one level to another. More black birds circled under a threatening sky and landed heavily on nearby roosts. Their eyes flickered.

'They're smaller here than in England.'

'Are they?'

'Which is surprising really since everything else seems bigger.'

Dorothea nodded slightly. She knew what he meant. It wasn't that the trees were any bigger or anything like that. It was just that the distances were greater and there was so much less in between. There was a feeling of weightlessness, of not being anchored anywhere. And in England people lived in towns and villages or on farms. They didn't live surrounded by forest unable to see what might emerge from it. It was that hemmed-in feeling she hated, and not knowing what lay in the bush that drove her to the beach.

Church looked at her again. She knew he was trying to think of something to say so she asked where he was from.

'Northamptonshire. My father was the squire at Brackley.'

'Our grandfather was a farmer near Elstead in Surrey.'

He nodded for her to continue. She shrugged.

'He lost all his land after the war.'

Mary threw away the twig she was using to scrape the sides of the pot. She got up and disappeared around the side of the hut. Church crossed his legs and uncrossed them. Dorothea rearranged her skirts. Surf rumbled in the distance. He sighed.

'I have never seen more barbarous-looking fellows.'

Dorothea smiled thinly.

He continued: 'Pray tell, what is a swell's son run out?'

'A gentleman's son who has spent his fortune.'

'I see.'

Dorothea pulled at a thread that was fraying the edge of her skirt. She wondered why he wore a black dress suit for travelling.

'I bought land on the Swan River. The men who said it was farming land were … were thieves. I brought seeds and plants from home. It would grow nothing. I'm sorry, you must excuse me.'

He blew his nose hard into his handkerchief. He had a long narrow face and pale eyes that protruded.

'So what did you do?'

'I decided to go to Van Diemen's Land. They tell me it is just like England. And I have an uncle there. Farming.'

He took a mouthful of tea.

⁓

The day being overcast made the hut look shabby, and the paperbark, which covered it, a dirty grey. Smoke rose from the granite stone chimney and drifted towards the clouds that bumped together above the sand ridge. She took off her shawl, feeling the weight of the air around her. Ants were crawling over her boots and when she looked closely the ground was moving. She stamped her feet and stood up. She looked for Mary as she reappeared from the well, wiping her hands on her gown.

'I'm going to the beach.'

Mary frowned.

'I want to,' she said irritably, and then seeing the look on her sister's face she added: 'Come on then.'

From the top of the granite they could see the outline of the mainland even though it seemed to be shrouded in rain, or was it smoke? She sat on a boulder and realised she had needed to remind herself that there was a mainland. Her sister carefully climbed up beside her. Sometimes Dorothea despaired of her. She wondered what Mary would do if it weren't for her. Perhaps she would just wait for someone else to tell her what to do. But it hadn't always been like that. There were seven children in their family, they were the oldest, only a year apart. The next was Jem who was four years younger. Dorothea and Mary had shared all their experiences, so when they were bad they were easier to bear. After they left England, Mary had been ill. They were all seasick but she was the worst, and even after she had recovered it was as though with all that heaving and retching she had vomited a part of herself into the sea. Their mother too seemed to have lost what life she had had in her. They had reacted to their new land like plants brought from England with root systems too weak to penetrate the hard soil. In the beginning it was Dorothea who had worked alongside Jem and their father to clear a small area of land so they could erect a tent.

When Matthew wanted Mary for his wife, Dorothea had been disturbed by her sister's lack of interest in what was happening to her. Looking back, though, she realised that their father probably wouldn't have allowed Mary to refuse him anyway. Dorothea hadn't wanted her sister to marry. She had watched Matthew one day when he came to visit. He couldn't see her because she was hanging the washing on the line that ran from the corner of the hut to the bush. He came upon her brother William who was kneeling at the front door step. The boy had carefully spread out his rock collection, lining up the small smooth oval ones and placing the colours together. As Matthew stepped he looked down and with one quick action kicked all the rocks off into the dirt. Dorothea knew too that something had happened between Jem and Matthew. Jem was only sixteen but he was solid and strong. Whatever it was, Matthew was quiet when he was around Jem.

Dorothea looked sideways at Mary and saw her own fear reflected in her eyes. As the sky darkened, the colours in the bay grew more intense and the smell of smoke and eucalyptus grew stronger. But the air was moist and suddenly there was no wind. Orange and yellow clouds edged the shadowy sky and brought with them thunder that rumbled through her and heightened her feeling of nervous anticipation. Then there were flashes of light, and foam and rumpled water as wind gusts tore across the bay. It was black as night as the ash sucked up by the storm wiped out the light. Then it rained. Black rain. Mary ran before her and they were running through spray that rose from the rock.

Church lit a lamp. They were sticky with moisture and fine dirt but at least they were sheltered. Church looked at them strangely for their bodies were outlined by wet hair and clothes. They couldn't find anything to wipe themselves with, so when Church left the room they lifted their skirts and wiped their faces with their undergarments. The fire threw out a golden glow and softened the edge of their fear.

Dorothea swept the floor with a branch she found by the door. It was hard to see into the corners and she startled a long black lizard with white markings. She gasped and Mary, who had been resting her head on her arms, jumped and lifted her feet off the ground as it shot into the other room. Dorothea stared after it and then continued to sweep, making patterns in the dirt. She reached the back wall and a ledge that ran about a foot below the ceiling where there were large cone and conch shells covered in dust and spiders' webs. Just inside the lip of the largest one was etched the figure of a naked woman. When she looked more closely she realised it was half woman, half seal.

Heavy footsteps crunched on the other side of the wall. The women looked at each other. Lighter footsteps followed. Men's voices murmured. Matthew and the boy burst into the hut. Like a dog, the boy shook his black curls.

'Brrr,' he growled.

'Christ! Wouldn't want to be at sea,' said Matthew.

Dorothea looked up. She thought it was so like him that somehow he wasn't with the rest of them.

'You were lucky I didn't tell them where you were.'

He ignored her and held out a canvas bundle in front of him. The boy, in a kangaroo-skin jacket, pushed beside him and laid his bundle on the table.

'Muttonbirds.'

'Muttonbird chicks. We got them in burrows on the other side of the island,' added Matthew.

He laid his bundle beside the boy's and untied the twine to reveal a mound of grey fluff. Dorothea reached across. Soft silky down covered the chick's still-warm body. When she turned it over, its broken neck flopped sideways. Dorothea looked up at the boy. He was standing at the end of the table. He nodded and grinned. She thought he was around the same age as their middle brother Charlie who was fourteen. She liked his eyes for they were direct and unusually coloured, tawny like a cat's. Matthew turned towards the door.

He spoke over his shoulder. 'Any sign of the sealers?'

Dorothea shook her head but asked whether there was anyone else who had been left behind on the island.

'Only him.' He nodded towards Church, who they could see through the doorway, sitting just under the verandah.

After they had plucked and gutted the birds they put them in a blackened pot with potatoes and turnips they had found in a barrel in the storeroom and hung it from a hook above the fire. As it simmered an oily sheen appeared and a strong fishy smell filled the hut and seemed to stick to their skin.

When she had something to do Dorothea was able to push the panic down. But as soon as she stopped and sat by the fire the sound of the waves seemed louder and stronger and the fear was harder to force down. She knew if she gave in to it, nothing would change. Suddenly the waves seemed much louder and she looked around and met Mary's startled gaze. But it was only thunder and the rain began again. First it was just heavy drops that plopped and tingged, but then a rush of water descended on the roof, leaking onto the table and floor.

The others returned to the kitchen. Matthew standing with his back to the fire, his hands clasped behind him, rocking backwards and forwards on his heels. Church found a chair against the wall. The boy flopped down in front of the fire, pulling his knees up and wrapping his arms around them. The rain roared. Yellow light of the fire lit their faces. Dorothea felt suspended in time and place. She found it impossible to imagine that outside their walls and over the sea were people. People living normal lives. Buying food at the store or grog at the inn.

Jem and Manning were the first to return. Dorothea had gone around to the back of the hut to bring in a pile of firewood which was now wet. She saw them through the trees. The rain had eased a bit and the sky had lightened, but still a hazy veil surrounded them. She noticed that drops had made patterns in the sand and when her boots sunk into it, they broke through the crust to the dry powdery stuff beneath. Manning was leading the way. He pushed back the branches and when he let go she could see the raindrops spray from the leaves. But the two lads didn't seem to notice. They sprang ahead, their feet scarcely touching the ground, stepping over the gullies of water that swept down from the rock.

'I ain't never heard of a shark breachin' like a whale,' called out Jem. 'Christ, it was a bigun.'

'Yeah.'

'See how it took that seal. I thought we was gone.'

'You thought you were gone, what about me?'

They disappeared around the other side of the hut. The cloud lifted and the hut shimmered through the gap in the trees. Leaves sparkled and Dorothea smelt the rich earth and the wet granite.

She looked into her brother's face and it was almost a stranger's. He didn't notice her either even though he was beside her in front of the fire. The sealers weren't far behind. Their voices filtered through the cracks in the wall and when they entered it seemed there wasn't the space to hold them. The rain paused. But the wind had picked up and it rustled the treetops.

The seal-oil lamp glowed dully in the smoky haze. Heat from the fire and damp unwashed bodies mingled with the stench of seal and cooked muttonbirds spread out on the table. They reached for bits of flesh-covered bone, their hands and faces shiny with grease. Dorothea's eyes watered and she almost choked on the rich odours but she ate like everyone else.

The door of the hut was pushed open and cool air freshened her face like a wet cloth. The black women, wearing skin cloaks over their shoulders, entered and placed seal flippers between sticks then held them over the flames, squatting at the feet of the men.

She caught words and snatches of sentences occasionally but most of the time the voices rumbled over and around her. Matthew held Mary close to him, his arm wrapped tightly around her waist. She couldn't see her sister's face for it was obscured by the hair that escaped from her comb.

'Bring in the Big Pup.'

The door to the storeroom opened and a keg of black-strap rum was rolled in and hacked open at the top. Mugs were dipped into the dark oily liquid. Everyone drank, even the black women and the boy. Someone sang a song. And someone fell over a chair at the back of the room. There was a scuffle. Voices got louder and the air more dense.

She was standing at the fire with Jem, swallowing the rich rum, her cheeks flushed and her eyes heavy.

'Did you get any seals, then?'

'What?' He couldn't hear her over the din.

'Seals!' she shouted. 'Did you get any?'

He nodded towards Manning.

'He did. Just about lost our whaleboat when we was trying to get off the island. Got pushed sideways and she almost went over. And there was this shark. It was longer than this room.'

She raised her eyebrows.

'It's the truth.'

He was almost daring her to contradict him. She recognised the defensive tone in his voice for she had heard it often enough after he had come home for good. In England he had lived with a wheelwright's family instead of his own. She knew he resented the fact that she and Mary had been able to stay home while he was sent away to work for someone else in another town. She wanted to say that she didn't disbelieve him, she was just surprised, but he had already turned away.

She stretched her hands towards the fire. Someone grabbed her arse. She swung around and looked down into Jansen's flushed face.

'Get off,' she said.

'I hope you haven't forgotten, my lovely.'

The men with Jansen watched with lascivious grins.

'Go on, if you ain't going to have her, I will.'

Words fell over other words and she could make no sense of them. Their faces came through the haze. There were many eyes, red-rimmed and glittering. She glanced over at Jem. He had his back to her and was speaking to Manning against the wall. Anderson and Isaac looked up from their cards. Another man, closer, reached for her skirts. It was one of Jansen's crew but she couldn't remember his name. She smoothed her gown and backed away towards the black women who watched curiously from the fire. Dulled by drink, she couldn't think. Where was Mary? With Matthew but now men stood between her and her sister. Her bodice felt tight across her chest and she found it difficult to breathe. She moved to the fireplace and shivered despite the heat. She could feel their eyes on her; it was like being poked in the back with a fire stick. Then something happened. She didn't know whether it was looking into the faces of the women by the fire or just being full of grog that did it. But she was angry. Seething, boiling, spewing with rage. She grabbed the poker that hung by the fireplace and faced them.

'Get away from me you dirty sons of bitches!' she screeched. She realised then it was easier to be angry than frightened. She shook her head as she waved the poker. Her hair loosened and fell in strands around her face. She was red and ugly. She glared at Jansen then at the others around the room. No one spoke. Between two men she caught a glimpse of Mary's head leaning on Matthew. Then someone started to laugh.

'You show them lass,' shouted a voice from the back.

'Aye.'

She froze then, uncertain what to do next. Waiting for one of them to lunge towards her. Slowly Anderson stood up. There was silence again. She let the poker drop to the ground. She watched the smirk slip off Jansen's face and he sunk towards the wall. Anderson pushed past the men in the doorway and opened the door. The rain had stopped but the air was brittle. He looked at her sideways and told her there was a pile of skins in the storeroom if she was cold.

~

From her nest of stinking fur she could see the line of light beneath the door. They were still drinking for she heard laughter. She tried not to think about the lizard that also lived there. The room was dry and warm but thick with dust. And things crawled beneath her.

January 1886

It was strange. Last night I had a dream about England. You were there beside Grandmother, playing with the ties of her bonnet, sucking your thumb and running the silky ribbon across the top of your lip. I am leaning against her shoulder and she is telling us a story about a prince and a princess. She smells of rosewater. We sit still on an old wooden chair even though we know there is no one to scold us for Grandfather is dead.

Then I leave Grandmother and I am older, walking the lane, which is edged on one side by a low stone wall, from her house to the town. It winds past the village hall where our mother had dancing lessons when she was a child. Then I reach the outskirts of town where they have built the big house for the poor. I see Grandmother's pale face in one of its mean little windows. Mother didn't want us to know. It is where Grandmother is to live after Father sells her house so we can sail to our new home.

Middle Island 1835, Dorothea Newell

The pool of clear water reflected the sun's progress as it rose from the other side of the island. The pool was a natural depression in the rock which had been deepened by the sealers. After they had lit a fire on the granite and the heat had split the rock, the men had dug out the fragments and built a wall at the lower end so that when it rained it would fill to a depth of about two or three feet. But that had been done before Dorothea arrived on the island. The rain over the past three weeks had filled it to capacity. She was sitting beside it, as she did most mornings. She squinted as the light brightened, for she was on the edge of the pool, facing it directly. The feathery pink dawn faded from its reflection.

The rock in front of her sloped down to the bush. To the left was the track to the camp but ahead was another track through the dense wattle to an inland lake she could glimpse over the treetops. Although salty it wasn't connected to the sea. The black women collected its salt for curing the skins. It was one of the main reasons the sealers made the island their base. As the sun moved further overhead the lake deepened in colour from a pale pink to a dusky rose. When she and her sister first discovered it, they were sure that it was a trick of the light. But when they stood on its spongy banks, the water rippled pinkly in front of them. Crystals lay below its surface and small shrimp flurried in its shallows. They held the water and it burnt the scratches on their hands.

Dorothea peered over the edge of the rock pool and stared hard at her reflection. Her eyes saw the outline of her head against the sky but then the image faded as her eyes focused beyond it to the strange translucent creatures that floated along the filmy bottom. Sometimes she wished she could disappear like her reflection. She felt like an animal that was being hunted but not in a way that was obvious. The hunter remained just beyond her vision. She sensed he was there and sometimes there was more than one. And the circles were getting smaller. She envied her sister for even though she didn't like Matthew, he at least shielded her from the eyes of the others.

In the first few days she really believed what she had said to Mary. That some vessel would pass by and they would sail east or west. She didn't care in which direction they went just as long as they were safe. But it was drawing close to winter. There would be no ships then. And Anderson wouldn't be taking them anywhere. She had overheard Jem and Manning. They said Anderson had threatened to kill Jansen for his boat.

She untied the twine that fastened a tammar skin around her shoulders. She took it off and laid it on the rock. She pulled up her sleeves, noticing the black grime under her fingernails. She cupped her hands and buried her face in the cold water, bringing the blood to her cheeks. After drying her face with a piece of rag, she pulled a comb through her hair. Usually she and her sister did each other's hair but today Mary had stayed in the tent. She wasn't hungry and she seemed more listless than usual. Dorothea knew it was easy to feel like that on the island. For often it seemed there was nothing to do. Time expanded and the only way to fill it was to watch the ants as they trickled through tiny pathways, crossing over sticks and leaves, from one side of the clearing to the other. Then other times there was food to prepare and plates to clean and firewood to collect and no sooner had they lit the fire in the morning than they were stoking it up for the night.

Hopefully, though, she wasn't with child. Dorothea tied her hair with a thin strip of leather. She met Dinah and Sal as they headed into the bush with snares for trapping tammar. If they saw her they showed no sign for they quickly vanished without a twig snapping or leaves rustling.

It was a clear, sharp morning. The sky had deepened to a dense blue. Black birds called to each other and wattle birds warbled and squabbled. The sea rumbled faintly in the distance. Smoke from the chimney hovered above the hut. Jem and Manning, unkempt wisps of hair framed in the golden light, sat cross-legged in the dirt facing each other with a skin on the ground between them. Jansen and two of the men from his boat were on the other side of the clearing. He seemed to be drawing something in the sand with a stick.

'Why aren't you sealing?' she asked Jem.

Her brother looked up, squinting. He was making a sheath for his knife like the one Manning wore on his belt. He put down the knife he had been using to punch holes with and shaded his eyes.

'Anderson's gone to the mainland in the other whaleboat.'

'Why?'

'For grasstree gum.'

'Why?'

Jem sighed and frowned, taking the knife again to the skin.

'Got a leak that's why. Stop asking me questions.'

'So who's gone with him?'

'Don't know. Isaac I think and a couple of the others.'

Mary came slowly around the side of the hut. Her hair was flattened on one side and her head was lowered. She looked up and smiled weakly when she saw her sister. Her eyes seemed darker than usual, or perhaps it was her skin that was paler.

A pot of water simmered in the fireplace. Mary sat down. Dorothea made tea from the ti-tree leaves they had collected. When Mary took the cup the sleeve of her gown slipped up, revealing red streaks that ran up her arm from her wrist.

'What's that?'

'What?'

'On your arm.'

Mary turned it around. Then Dorothea noticed the weeping sore between her thumb and forefinger.

'How did you get that?'

Mary shrugged.

'How long have you had it?'

'Oh, I don't know.' She pulled her hand away and turned her head. 'It doesn't matter.'

'What's wrong with you? Give it here and I'll clean it.'

'It'll be alright.'

'Don't be silly.'

Dorothea took her arm and laid it on the table. Mary's wrist was hot. She dipped a rag in hot water and bathed the sore, wiping away the yellow crust. Mary winced. Dorothea shook her head. Neither of them noticed Mooney. When Mary looked up she saw her staring at her hand. Their eyes met and Mooney backed away. Dorothea smelt her musky campfire smell and turned around, noticing briefly the brownish mud in her hair and the chalky markings on the back of her arms and legs. She kept cleaning Mary's hand.

Then Mooney returned from the fire and held out her hand. In the middle of her palm was a grey greasy substance. She gestured with her other hand.

'She's saying rub it on,' said Dorothea.

Mary pulled her arm away and glared at Mooney who quickly cast her eyes to the floor and backed away. Dorothea stared after her.

'You should try it.'

'What?'

'Well it could work. They must have their own remedies. How do they survive in the bush?'

'They don't. They're dying all the time.'

But Dorothea had got up from the table and was standing over Mooney, watching her rub the salve into her own skin.

'A little bit,' she said, holding her thumb and forefinger together.

Mooney froze for a moment and then held out her finger. Dorothea scraped some of it from her skin and returned to her seat at the table. She put her finger under her nose. It smelt of smoke and animal fat.

'I ain't having it,' said Mary shaking her head. She held her hands out in front of her as though to push Dorothea away.

'Just try it.'

'I don't need to.' Mary stood up, moving out from behind the table. 'And I don't need you always telling me what to do!'

Dorothea stared after her. She was surprised for she hadn't heard Mary speak like that for a long time. She was pleased in a way for it showed she cared about something. But there was something else in her voice beside the frustration that Dorothea knew they both felt. It was hostility. Was it towards her? The sun cast rectangular light on the floor and lit bits of fluff in the air as they floated, some gently downwards, others spiralling dramatically. She turned away, her eyes now un-accustomed to the gloom. Mooney had become a formless shape by the fire.

Jansen's bulk filled the doorway, his two men behind him. They scraped the dirt with their feet and roughly pushed the chairs away from the table. She knew he wouldn't have entered had Anderson been there. She ignored them.

'Make us a tea, my lovely.'

The other two smiled sickly. From the corner of her eye she noticed Mooney slip outside.

'Get it yourself … Anyway, what are you doing here? If Anderson sees you, he'll have you.'

Jansen moved his thick forearm across the table, sliding it back and forth.

'Aye. He won't be back for a while and we got important things to discuss.'

Dorothea raised her eyebrows.

'So … get us a cup of tea.'

She got up from the table and poured tea into three cups.

'So what are you up to then?'

Jansen looked across the table at the other two men.

'Perfect weather for sailing.'

'There's no wind,' said Dorothea as she pushed a cup towards him.

'Aye 'tis changing … it'll be from the east by morning.'

His face was raw and his lower lip black from bleeding blisters. He brought the tea up to his mouth but before he swallowed he cleared his throat and spat sideways onto the floor. Light shone through the gaps in the wall and striped their faces. They drained the contents of their cups. Black creased knuckles, yellowed and broken nails.

'Are you leaving?' she asked.

He studied her and wiped the whiskers above his mouth with his hand. She thought there had probably been a time when he had been considered handsome, but the grog had reddened his skin and clouded his eyes.

'You can't tell anyone. Not even that sister.'

'What is it?' she asked. 'Are you leaving us here?'

He leant back and folded his arms behind his head. Eyes narrowed.

'Could take you, I suppose. What do you think lads?'

'Anderson'll kill you if he finds out.'

'He ain't going to, is he?'

She looked down at her hands that were holding the edge of the table. Her knuckles were white. She wanted to leave the island. They all wanted to. But she couldn't leave her sister. And besides, did she really trust Jansen to make it back to the Sound?

'Who are you taking?'

'You don't know anything.'

He reached over and wrapped his coarse fingers around her wrist. He grinned and his eyes were sparkling slits. She tried to pull away but he held more tightly. They laughed as she struggled some more. Finally he let go but not before he had pressed hard enough to leave red welts on her skin. She turned away from the table, rubbing her wrist.

⁓

She struggled to get the lid off the keg of flour. She left the storeroom for a knife and returned. It was musty and lit only by a gap between the walls and the eaves. Drums and two large chests were against the wall and on the floor was a pile of kangaroo, tammar and seal skins. Rope and twine of twisted grass and roo tendons lay coiled amongst them. She prised the keg open. It was the flour saved from the *Mountaineer*. How long would she be on the island if she didn't leave with Jansen? It seemed that supplies were low. They brewed ti-tree leaves instead of tea. Men were running out of tobacco. But the vegetable seedlings were sprouting in the garden.

She returned to the kitchen with her bowl of flour. By the fire she picked out the maggots. They sizzled as they hit the coals. She remembered being in the inn with her sister and Matthew. They had just returned from organising their passage on the *Mountaineer* and Captain Jansen had arranged to meet them. She didn't realise that Matthew had promised to introduce her. Jansen was clean-shaven then, except for a ginger moustache which he waxed at the ends, and his eyes were clear and the palest blue. He had looked into her eyes instead of letting them wander over her face and her neck and her chest. So she had listened and smiled. There was nothing for her at the Sound. After they set sail she realised her mistake. He was no different from the others. In fact she would've been surprised if he had even bought her a gown. Thankfully he had left her alone on the island but she guessed it was because he hadn't wanted to draw attention to himself. He was such a fool, she thought. Why had he brought them here? He must have known what another boat was worth to a sealer.

She poured some water from the pail into the flour. With the bowl nestled between her thighs, she plunged her hands into the mixture, squeezing it between her fingers. She widened her hands and took in the whole mass, punching and rolling and working it into a stiff dough. She glanced over her shoulder. Jansen was watching. She clenched her teeth and took the dough out of the bowl. She laid it on the cloth that was the reverse side of a kangaroo skin. She shaped the dough into a loaf of about four inches by eight inches then brushed it with dry flour. Then she dug out a hole in the fireplace and placed the loaf in it, covering the top with hot ashes.

The smell of bread baking filled the air. It wafted through the camp and brought the men through the door like flies to rotting meat. She wiped her hands on her skirts and pushed back the strands of hair that were stuck to her face. Matthew entered, followed by Church. She hadn't seen Church since the fight. It hadn't really been a fight, more like a performance by one of Jansen's crew who had it in for Church. One afternoon she and her sister had come through the trees to find Church on his back in the dirt. The man was standing over him. Men were jeering and joking. The man had a knife that was long and curved and it flashed when he twirled it with both hands above his head. He pointed it towards Church, the body in black. The man's face was expressionless except for his eyes. They were bright with excitement. The tip caught the fabric of the stock and he hooked it slowly and it tore. Everyone watched Church's eyes roll around in their sockets. She was unable to move. She had almost wanted to clap as though she'd just witnessed the act of a street performer. Afterwards she knew she hadn't wanted him hurt, but when Mead stopped the man from going any further, she had felt almost as disappointed as the rest of them. The cut on Church's face was still raw. He would be left with a scar. Church took a seat at the end of the table. She wondered if he knew of Jansen's plans. Matthew sat against the wall. He looked around nervously as though he was expecting something to happen.

⁓

Church laid a stack of paperbark on the table and placed a limpet shell beside it. He filled the shell with thick, bright red liquid from a small flask. He also took from his pocket the quill of a big gull. Dorothea stood over him.

'What's that?' she asked.

'Seal's blood, I'm going to write in seal's blood,' he said.

Dorothea looked at Matthew. He shrugged his shoulders. Jansen heard and laughed unpleasantly.

'What are you writing? Help?'

The others sniggered.

Dorothea picked up a sheet of paperbark. It was soft and

spongy and cream coloured. On the other side were pink fibres. Gently she prised the creamy layers apart into single sheets that were clean and firm.

'What are you going to write?'

'I don't know,' he said. 'Something, perhaps, about where we are.'

January 1886

George and I were married only ten years ago. Does that surprise you? I was fifty-nine years old before I was married in a church. It was the Wesleyan Church behind my house in Duke Street. I wore a gown of white merino with a white satin bonnet and full. George also bought me a China crepe shawl which hangs behind the door.

Middle Island 1835, James Manning

Manning pretended to look away when Dorothea spoke to Jem. But he watched her from the corner of his eye and then more openly as she turned and followed her sister into the hut. She walked with a straight back, her hair swaying across her shoulders. He swallowed loudly and turned his attention to Jem who was bent over a piece of skin. He frowned and decided that Jem was useless. He took the piece of skin from his hands.

'Here, like this.'

He poked the leather strip through the hole using the tip of his knife. He handed it back to Jem who took it, but when he looked down, hair fell into his eyes. Irritated, Jem pushed the curls off his face. But they continued to fall into his eyes. So with the knife he hacked off his fringe and brushed the hair from his knees.

Manning glimpsed someone hovering behind a wattle tree at the edge of the clearing. He remained out of sight until Manning decided he must have gone. But then he saw his head around one side looking behind the camp. It was that rat, Owens. The bastard was up to something. Then he noticed the young boy coming down through the trees from the granite. He passed Owens and continued towards the beach. Owens was visible now. He seemed to be waiting. Shifting his balance from one leg to another. He looked towards the hut and saw Manning. Manning turned away. When he looked up again, Owens had gone.

'Jem …'

Jem's mouth was twisted and he frowned as he concentrated.

'What?'

'I've got to see what that bastard's up to.'

'Who?'

'That bleedin' rat.'

Manning sprang up. When Jem looked up he had disappeared between the trees.

⁓

A thread of foam moved back and forth over shiny sand. Beyond it the sea was a rippling turquoise, darkening in places where weed lay beneath the surface, and then it was an inky blue. The hills of Mount Arid stood clearly defined and the break on the edge of the cape flashed white. Crystal wavelets rose and lapped gently at the rock's edge. They swept over ribbons and broad-leafed weed that swayed with the current. He watched his step for the rock was uneven. He had knocked the skin off his toes so many times that the sores wouldn't heal. He caught a glimpse of Owens as he rounded the headland. He paused, waiting for Jem.

By the time they reached the seaweed beach there were only footprints on the sand between the brown lumps. The sea had arranged its discarded weed in piles a couple of feet high and over a distance of about twenty feet or more. They were thick bunches of ribbon that dried grey on top and that crackled as their feet sank into it. Occasionally they'd step on the sharp edge of a shell, and sometimes they'd catch the smell of something rank as though a fish had been trapped in its net.

They reached the end of the beach and faced Flinders Peak, both breathing heavily. Manning glimpsed the bobbing head of Owens as he climbed over the rocks at the other end of the next beach. Sweat was stinging his eyes. The sharp edge of the rocks in front of him softened and wavered and the sun on the water sparkled. He paused for a moment. And then an image he had tried to bury rose up in his mind. He remembered the feeling of his backbone pressed against the foremast. He had been looking for a place to hide. But he knew the way below was blocked. The ship was pitching and he got down on his hands and knees and crawled across to the forehatch, carefully lowering himself down. He looked up and the light from below contorted the rat-like features into a face from hell. The pain from Owens standing on his fingers was nothing compared to what he knew would come later.

Manning set his jaw.

'Come on,' he muttered.

Jem frowned.

'What?'

'Watch me back.'

They passed Anderson's overturned whaleboat and the dorsal fin of a shark that poked up out of the sand. Anderson had shot it the last time they were sealing. The shark had measured twelve feet and three inches long and eight feet round. They tied rope around its tail and towed it behind them. It attracted other sharks, which they shot and left in the sea to sink slowly, white bellies disappearing into red clouds. They pulled it to shore and slit its stomach, releasing the pungent smell of ammonia from its gut and the remains of a seal bitten in two with a spear through it. They cleaned the shark and cut away the fillets, leaving its fins and grey rubbery skin part-buried in the sand.

Manning and Jem reached the end of the beach. Owens had vanished. They climbed onto splinters of basalt rock lying on larger slabs of rock. In some places creamy quartz ran in thick ribbons over the uneven surface. There was still no sign of him. They left the black and white rock and came down onto another beach almost at the base of Flinders Peak. Thick vegetation ran steeply up the side of the hill until it reached the stripy granite. Higher up were thick gashes in the rock where lizards and bats and birds hid amongst the caves and ledges and crevices.

They thought they had lost him. They retraced their steps and then Jem saw two sets of prints higher up close to the thick scrub. Their feet sank into soft warm sand that after a while was wearing on their lower legs. The beach dipped where once a small creek had run down from the hill. The footprints vanished. They stopped. Jem was about to say something but Manning turned and grabbed his arm and put a finger to his lips.

'Listen!'

Jem listened but he could only hear the hooting of a bronze-wing pigeon and the occasional squawk of a gull that wheeled above and around the towering face of the nearby rock. Manning motioned for him to follow. They got down on their hands and knees and crawled under the sticks and branches that crisscrossed the dry creek bed. Water couldn't have run there for a long time for although it cut sharply into the sandhill it was choked with debris. Marks in the dirt showed that Owens had been there, dragging something behind him. They rounded the bend, and Manning who was ahead suddenly sank back on his heels. He nodded in that direction.

'They're here.'

'Who?' whispered Jem.

'Shush!'

Manning took the knife from his belt. Jem watched him and felt for his own. Then he remembered he had left it back at the camp. But before he could say anything, Manning sprang upwards and ran, crashing and leaping through undergrowth and down onto a man whose trousers were around his ankles.

After they had cut the boy free he ran into the bush. Manning and Jem weren't saying anything to each other. They ambled along the beach at the base of the big rock. The sea sparkled in the channel between Flinders Peak and Goose Island. Manning knew that even though he had wanted to kill Owens he couldn't. He glanced sideways at Jem who walked with his eyes on the ground. He swung his right arm backwards and forwards, holding his shoulder with his other hand. It felt as though it had been wrenched from its socket and his back ached. He realised he ached all over. And the bastard had grabbed him around the waist, catching his fingers in his money belt. Manning put his hand under his shirt. The belt was loose so he tightened it.

Jem still wasn't saying anything. Manning watched him pick up a stone and cast it out into the water. It skimmed the surface and bounced two or three times before it plopped and drew perfect circles that grew and grew. Manning picked up a rock too. It fitted in the palm of his hand, smooth and oval. He stroked it with his fingers for it felt nice and hot. He flicked his wrist and sent it skimming across the water, where it hopped several times before landing with a plop. Jem looked up and grinned. They hunted around for more rocks.

Much later they sat in the sand facing the sea and were warmed by the low afternoon sun.

'The *Defiance* ... she was a dirty miserable schooner. The skipper, his name was Merredith. He was buying skins off the sealers. He said he was sailing for Swan River.'

Manning drew patterns in the sand with his finger.

'Didn't get far. Left Sydney in August two years ago. We passed Cape Howe and the wind headed us and turned to a gale. We were blown off the land. She blew like one of them hurricanes. We were hove-to. The skipper said she ain't going to stand up much longer. The sea is rising. The wind'll be worse when the moon gets up. So we brought down the topmast and she lay-to a bit easier.'

Manning paused, remembering.

'But the waves, you ain't never seen anything ... they had curling monster heads, and they was like hills rising up and when we were in the hollow it was quiet. You couldn't even hear the screeching of the wind. The helm was lashed and they was all below 'cept me. I was on deck for they couldn't get me there. Them bastards scared witless. I prayed she'd break up

and they'd be the first to get their bleedin' feet wet. I didn't
care what happened.'

They listened to the gentle sigh of the ocean as its waves
slapped the sand and swept it in half-circles all the way along
the beach. The sun was retreating quickly and the sand
beneath them was cold. Jem rubbed his arms. About half a
mile back they saw Owens stumble out of the bush, his shirt
torn and flapping behind him. When they couldn't see him
any longer they got to their feet and headed back to the camp.
The air grew cold as the sun sunk further. They wandered, two
small figures against an immense backdrop of wispy strands of
coloured cloud in a lavender sky and a dark velvet sea that
spread out to surround distant islands.

He pushed back the thin branches that crossed his path. He
could hear Jem trampling heavily behind him. Wet air had
descended into the hollow and the sticks he fought back were
slimy to touch. They came out into the other clearing and saw
firelight winking through tangled wattle. It was the black
women's camp. The dark shape of a woman glided before the
fire. Manning stopped.

'What are you doing?'

Jem came up against him.

'There's no one about,' said Manning uneasily.

Jem shrugged and they continued to the hut. Manning
stood back as Jem went before him. The air was dry and smelt
of smoke and damper. Dorothea and Mary looked up.

He stood with his back to the fire, staring into the dark
corners of the hut. He felt her eyes on him. He registered her

appearance, her soiled gown and her bare, blackened feet. She was like all the dirty whores he knew. There was one who had been kind to him once. It was his mother. But he never thought of her because she was dead. He had been taught to hate her and other women like her when he began working with mariners.

'Look like you fell into a bush.' Dorothea glanced at him and then towards her sister who smiled.

He knew it. They were making fun of him. He turned back to the fire, warming his hands and relishing the heat on his legs. He would show her who she could laugh at.

When he could smell his trousers singeing he left to stand in the doorway. From there he could hear snatches of coarse voices from over the sandhill. Anderson had returned from the mainland and the others must have been down on the beach. Lights appeared, glowing torches held above the heads of solid shapes on the crest of the dune. Behind them the sky was yellow and purple where the sun had not long set. Slung between the featureless men were two large kangaroos. They were dumped in the middle of the clearing and the animals' ungainly legs sprang up and fell sideways.

Jem came up behind him and they both moved outside to get a better look. One of the men pointed his torch at a pile of firewood. Yellow tongues licked at the kindling. Faces glowed and flickered. Anderson pushed between Dorothea and Mary who stood in the doorway and then came back with a knife. Its blade caught the reflection of dancing flames. Smooth white wood was thrown on top of the fire and devoured by a shower of sparks and long tendrils of light. Balls of smoke rolled into the air and drifted randomly, stinging eyes and choking throats. Men and women drew closer like moths to its fiery brightness.

Anderson leant over a kangaroo and cut through its fur. He parted the hide from the body as though he were peeling the skin of a vegetable and threw it aside. The strange triangular body of the naked kangaroo gleamed white in the light and was marked with a web of purple veins. He cut a slit in the flesh of a hind leg and drew out of it a long white tendon. He wound it around his wrist and then reached for the other leg. Thick ropy muscles bulged from his forearms and his forehead shone. Shadows deepened the lines between his eyes and around his mouth. He stood up and straightened his back and then reached down again to cut through the taut skin of the belly, releasing its contents, like water bursting from a split in a water bag. He fastened back the sides of the stomach with wooden skewers and pulled out the steaming slippery coils of intestines. The black women who had been standing in the shadows came forward. They placed the guts onto the coals they had flicked out from their own fire and used sticks to turn them over.

The air was rich with the sizzling smell of meat roasting. The animal's heart and liver were baked in its chest. Sparks spat out from the fire. Owens stood up and Manning noticed the blood crusted on his face and his swollen eye. He waited for him to look towards him but he didn't. Someone put more wood on the fire and a shower of orange light shot up and lit the low bush and the thin pale trunks behind them. Smoke surged towards him and it felt as though his eyeballs would melt. But when he moved away, the cold air embraced him so he quickly shuffled back.

His eyes were drawn to the bright coals. He thought he could see a face or perhaps it was more like a skull. An eye socket glared red and then turned grey and disintegrated as a log collapsed above it. He felt warm and well fed. It was enough. He felt like a moth that had broken from its cocoon, emerging in a new skin, discarding the old that had been worn by the lad. Many hours at an oar had brought its reward. He straightened his arms, satisfied by the ache in his muscles. He breathed deeply and glanced around at the firelit faces. They wouldn't cross him now.

He was conscious of Jem's presence beside him. His head rested on his arms and he closed his eyes but he could still see the dull glow of the fire. Then he noticed voices behind him. For some reason they made him uneasy. But before he could turn around something flashed in front of him and then he felt it, cold under his chin. He sensed faces turned towards him. Movement behind him and pain in his back, dense and solid, which spread. Someone had kicked him. He grunted and fell into the knife. The blade burnt. He closed his eyes and swallowed the darkness. His head was wrenched back by a hand clasped to his hair. The blood on his neck cooled and he looked up into the eyes of Anderson.

'No one steals, not on my island.'

Head wrenched further back until he thought his neck would snap. Finding it difficult to breathe. Suddenly he was let go. His head flopped forward and he shook his hair. He reached up to his neck and ran his hand over the scratch that was wet. Glancing on the ground behind him, he saw Anderson's broad feet.

'I ain't done yet. You stole from him.'

'Hey.' He turned towards Anderson and saw for the first time Owens beside him. 'I didn't steal off him. He's lying!' He looked over at Jem. 'That's the truth ain't it?'

Jem nodded, looking around nervously.

'You'd be a lying little snake for as I reckon you got his money.' Anderson turned to Owens. 'How much does he owe you?'

Owens cleared his throat and his good eye narrowed.

'I ain't sure. About four quid, I reckon.'

Manning brought a hand up to his waist.

'No it's mine! It's me savings.'

'Give it up or I'll slice it off and it won't be all I'll be slicing.'

Manning looked back towards the fire, seeing briefly the way Owens had cringed before him that afternoon. He sighed bitterly. He stood up and glared with hatred at both of them. At least Owens glanced away but Anderson just stared back. He pulled the belt from under his shirt and handed it to Anderson. The fire crackled. Anderson entered the hut with Owens and Isaac. A few minutes later he returned and tossed the belt back to him.

Manning left the fire, the sound of men's laughter echoing in his head. He scuffed the damp sand with his feet and brought a cold hand up under his shirt and retied the belt around his waist. There was a slither of light from the moon glinting on the liquid surface. The foam on the edge of the wave looked like the white scalloped frill of a petticoat that was pulled back and forth over the sand. It swirled around his toes and felt warmer than his blood. He tore a strip from his trouser leg, dipped it in the sea and wiped his neck. It stung at first but he knew it was only a shallow cut. He tossed the piece of rag away then ripped another strip from his pants and tied it around his neck. He held his battered hands out in front of him. The skin had split between his knuckles. He turned them over and felt the hard lumps of scar tissue that had misshapen his palms. He rubbed them together for they were cold and then he buried his face in them. The hardest thing was he knew why Anderson didn't believe him. He told him he had lost his money when the *Defiance* was wrecked because if he hadn't someone would have found a way to take it off him.

He noticed on his way back that there were a pile of skins and two barrels hidden in a sand hollow. Instead of taking the track, he had come up through the bush to the clearing. Jem lifted his head briefly as Manning settled but he didn't say anything.

After he had unrolled his bedding Manning looked up at the clear night sky. White pinpricks of light were arranged in misty clusters. The stars more bright and sharply defined than ever. The Southern Cross winked above him and it reminded him of another time he had lain awake looking at the stars. He was in the bilge of a whaleboat, his head resting against the seat trying to sleep. The swell dropped off. Instead of being rolled around at the bottom of the boat, which rubbed raw the sores on his body, the sea gently rocked him. He knew then that they must be close to land.

It had been five months since they had left the wreckage of the *Defiance* on the beach near Cape Howe. They had sailed close to the coast, hauling up occasionally for water and game. Now it was close to the end. The two Negroes they had collected along the way, Bathurst and Brown, lay at the bottom of the boat and lifted their heads. They woke the Dutchman and Captain Merredith, asleep at the steering oar. Land-ho. The two black women also stirred. The sky lightened to reveal a metal-grey sea and a deep indented bay lined with red mud cliffs. They took to the oars and rowed alongside them until they reached a small rocky point on the northeastern side of Kangaroo Island.

They made camp in the gully away from the rust-coloured boulders that lined the water's edge. A few days later they built a hut. Brown had been a ship's carpenter on an American whaler. They cut through the thick scrub behind the camp to the tall timber that grew in a valley about a mile away. While they worked Brown told Manning how he and Bathurst had deserted their ship. They stole a whaleboat and along with three other hands headed for the coast only to be swamped by a wave. Brown and Bathurst swam ashore. They didn't know what had happened to the others.

The black women kept them fed on a diet of small emu and kangaroo. Merredith had taken them aboard his vessel to trade them for skins. But since they were shipwrecked before they reached any sealers he took one of them for his wife. After she lay too close to the fire and burnt her leg, he called her Bumblefoot. For a while Manning lost track of time. There was always plenty of food and most of the time he was left alone. But he never lost sight of his goal, which was to reach Swan River.

He had liked the old Dutchman. They used to sit away from the others under a thick gum, and over the noisy chatter of the pink and grey birds, the Dutchman would tell him stories of being on an English man-o'-war. The old man had fought in the French Revolutionary Wars. His ship mutinied when the captain gave them five-water grog instead of three-water. The weather was bitter he said, and no man could endure it on a spirit so thin.

Sometimes their neighbours would haul up on the beach in front of the camp. They would only ever come by sea for inland was a knotted mess of impenetrable scrub. Many had lived on Kangaroo Island for years. Clothed in skins of all sorts, with sealskin caps and matted manes of hair, they would come ashore on battered whaleboats with greasy canvas strung tight above the gunwales. Often they would have with them three or four black women and dogs. The first time they visited Manning noticed that the women had bits of their ears cut off. Then one day he saw one of the sealers crop the top of his woman's ear when he thought she was too slow getting his flask from the boat. When they left, Merredith would put away his musket. Then he would release Bumblefoot and the other one from the hut where they had been hidden with the precious pile of skins.

Manning remembered the day it all changed. It was late afternoon and the sea rippled red and silver like molten metal. He was looking east, where a thick strip of land stretched across the water, and behind it, lit by the sinking sun, was the mainland, when a whaleboat came into view as it rounded the point from American River. Its six oars dipped into the sea and orange light followed the ripples as they fanned out from the bow and sparkled. The man on the seventh oar, standing at the stern, steered the boat towards the camp. A dirty sail hung limply above their heads. Manning could see it was overburdened with men, women, dogs and supplies. As it scraped the rocky bottom, most of them jumped out into the shallows and waded towards the hut. Manning, who was higher up in the bush, watched uneasily. He saw the old Dutchman come out to greet them. Merredith and Brown followed. There was a shout from the black man in a red shirt with a black bandana around his neck. He and Brown slapped each other on the back and the stranger punched the air with his fist. Manning didn't know it then but it was Anderson.

He leant up against the rough bark of the eucalypt behind him and watched as they unloaded the whaleboat. Anderson waded back and forth through the water. His wet trousers clinging to the powerful shape of his legs. He hoisted a barrel from the boat and slung it across his shoulders. Suddenly Bathurst crashed through the undergrowth near Manning.

'Hey, what's up?'

'We got visitors.'

'Well I'll be …' Bathurst caught sight of Anderson. 'Hey brother!' Anderson looked up and his face slowly opened into a smile.

Manning was never sure whether Bathurst and Brown had known Anderson before then. They called each other brother but he never heard them talking about being on the same ship. That night, however, Manning realised he would have to be careful. No man was as well armed as Anderson, and his men didn't seem to be with him by choice. He listened carefully though when Anderson started to talk of his plans to head west. There were islands there, he said, with water and wallaby and thousands of fur seal. But first Anderson said he had to build another boat. And over the weeks that followed that was what he did, using the native pine, and she-oak and eucalypt that grew in the scrub behind them.

Manning watched Anderson. He took on the role of leader and nobody disputed it. At the time he had hair that was tightly curled against his skull. And unlike the others, he shaved occasionally. He never said much and he didn't need to. There were always people willing to do his work for him. Especially Bathurst and Brown who obeyed him like he had royal blood or something. Despite his size he was agile. If he sensed someone behind him he would spring quickly and quietly so that it was the other person who was taken by surprise. And he would face them then with either one or both his guns. He couldn't have been long off a ship for his clothes weren't worn. Manning overheard him talking about the Kent Group of islands, which he knew were in the Bass Strait, but that was all he gave away. And the old Dutchman didn't know anything about him either.

He decided to risk it. He offered to work for Anderson if he would take him when he went west. Anderson worked a chaw of tobacco around in his mouth, spitting to the side. He said he could work for rations, which had suited Manning at the time. Manning discovered he hated sealing and that he hated the men who were sealers. He was always cold and stinking and the others would force him to do things they wouldn't do themselves, like going over the side of a cliff to get to the seals below. One of the men lost a finger. It swelled up and went red and so his brother cut it off. Meanwhile Anderson showed no sign of leaving. They kept working the islands, Thistle and Boston. And then sometimes they would raid the mainland for women. When he asked, Anderson would say soon enough. And then one day when Manning refused to work any more, Anderson put a gun to his head.

They were back at Kangaroo Island when Captain Jansen sailed the *Mountaineer* into the bay. Merredith knew Jansen, for he was another seal trader. He brought with him plenty of grog, which Anderson's men took for payment for their share of the skins. Everyone was drunk for a few days and although Manning couldn't recall much later, he remembered Anderson's face when Dinah told him the new whaleboat had gone. Manning thought Anderson was going to skin her. His skin paled and the scar beneath his eye gleamed. His nostrils flared and he stood very still with his knife pointed at her gullet. Manning felt like curling into the ground like the strange spiky creatures they sometimes found on the island. But Anderson just flicked his knife into the trunk of a nearby tree and Dinah turned away. Then he called after her, who was gone? When he pulled the knife from the bark the look on his face was dreadful for he learnt that Bathurst and Brown were amongst them. They left behind three men and three women and a boy.

Manning discovered Jansen was leaving for King George Sound and he paid him three pounds for a passage. It wasn't until they were loading the boat with barrels of water that he learnt Anderson had done a deal with Jansen to get his men and his boat to Middle Island. On their voyage across the dark expanse of sea Jansen was drunk all the time and so Manning stayed with Anderson on Middle Island.

But Jansen had made it to the Sound. If he had gone with him perhaps he'd be at Swan River now. The place so keenly etched in his mind. He had first heard of it from a sailor who had brought settlers from England to the new colony. He talked of still waters and black swans. Green valleys and tall trees. It couldn't be more different from Sydney he said. There were no mean-eyed bastards to trip you up and loose women to steal your money. It was clean and the land was cheap. That night when Manning entered his lodgings it was raining and sewage had flooded the bottom floor. He decided then that he would save his money and work his way there.

But his luck was rotten. First it was the bastards on the *Defiance*. Men so depraved they could have been animals. Just as he welcomed the notion of drowning, he was saved from the sea and transported from one island to the next. He had thought then that at least he was heading in the right direction and that he still had his money. But now he couldn't even say that. He tossed about in his swag of skins and hoped that his loathing would leak into Anderson's consciousness and that he would know that one day he was going to get what he deserved. He was momentarily comforted by that idea and his mind slipped into his body's exhaustion and soon he was asleep.

Manning and Jem looked down from the top of the world. Or it felt like that from the rounded mound of Flinders Peak for it was the highest point for miles. An icy breeze from the south cooled their faces and ruffled the surface of the ocean. For the first time they could see the shape of their island, its deep bays and thin points that trailed out into the sea, and it looked from where they stood like the piece of a puzzle. It was smaller than they thought. The oval pink lake, surrounded by a grey crust, was like an open wound amongst thick green scrub. Then above and below and in every direction the sky and the sea, two tones of the same colour, meeting along an indistinct curve until occasionally another rock like the one they stood on rose up and out of the water to break the pattern. Slick paths of silver ran across the sea like snail trails and foam flashed white on its edge. The mainland coast was so close they could see the stripe of the beach. From it grey bush like a coarse fabric covered the lumpy contours of the land and tucked into purple rock. A thin line of cloud lay along the pale edge of the sky. And overhead the infinite space deepened to a dense blue with the occasional thread of wispy mist.

Jem spun around and around, laughing and squinting against the blue that wrapped around them, until he fell over.

'Look out, you'll fall off.'

But Manning grinned too. He decided that if there was a God, then that was where He would be. He didn't think much of religion, for anyone he had met who knew about it made him think that it wasn't worth getting into. He twirled slowly around, squinting too but in effort to see any sign of human life. He could see many miles to the south and the east and the west so that had there been a ship passing, he was sure to be able to see it. He grabbed Jem's arm.

'Look, quick! There!'

A single sail above a small boat flickered white, just on the other side of Goose Island, to the west. Perhaps it was Anderson. But they knew he was caulking his boat for they could see smoke from the fire on the beach. It had to be the *Mountaineer's* whaleboat.

'Mother of Jesus! You know what that means, don't you?'

Manning looked at Jem, shading his eyes from the sun. Jem shook his head. His lip seemed to stick out further than normal and his hair, which he had hacked off, framed his face in ugly spikes.

'That's Jansen. The bastard's gone.'

Manning hit the rock as hard as he could with his stick. It didn't break for it was hardwood they had cut for clubbing seals. They had gone to the base of the rock to cut the clubs that morning and then decided to push their way through the scrub to see the view from the top. As he swung it he felt the pain in his back where Anderson had kneed him and it seemed to expand into his chest so that he could hardly breathe. He was aware of Jem and he turned into the wind and wiped the corners of his eyes. Then he sat down. He knew Anderson would be furious. Another whaleboat gone. Bitterly, he wondered who had escaped this time.

'We have to do something.'

'What?' asked Jem.

They faced west, towards the Sound.

'Keep coming back here until a ship passes and then signal them.'

'How?' asked Jem as he watched a sea eagle hover in the air in front of him and dive deep and straight down the rock face to the sea below.

'Fire.'

'Think it was blacks.'

Manning scraped the crumbly surface of a small indentation in the rock with the end of his club.

'We could build a boat.'

'Build a boat?'

'I saw him on Kangaroo Island.'

He nodded towards the beach where they both knew Anderson was. Jem didn't speak. They could hear the roar of the sea as it broke on the steep southern side of the island. Manning looked at his friend and suddenly he wasn't sure about him.

'You want to leave, don't you?'

Jem nodded. 'But I want me share.'

'He ain't going to give it to you.'

'What do you mean?'

'I mean he ain't going to pay me or you.'

'How do you know?'

'Because I know that filthy bastard.'

They were both silent for a moment, the wind parting their hair on the backs of their heads. The breeze had increased and moved into the southeast. There was a band of cloud that was thickening above the mainland and to the east. Manning was suddenly glad he wasn't in Jansen's whaleboat that morning. His eye followed the coast as it curved from the purple hills of Mount Arid to the flat line of beach that continued for miles.

'You know, we could get him to put us across there.'

'And then what?'

'We walk. It ain't that far.'

'Thistle Cove took three days sailing.'

'Be quicker, us walking.' He poked his stick towards the coast. 'Look there, we just follow the coast. Easy, can't get lost.'

Jem followed Manning's gaze.

'Yeah.' He ran his fingers over his mouth, sighed and then said: 'We'll need a gun.'

'Of course and we'll get it, even if we have to steal it.'

Manning stood up and rubbed his hands together to get rid of the little loose stones that stuck to his palms.

'When?'

'Come on, we'll go see Anderson.'

Jem frowned. 'Now?'

But Manning was already clambering down the rock.

January 1886

I see their faces at night. They open their mouths like beached fish but I can't hear what they're saying. When Mother died she looked like a blowfish. The doctor peeled her fingers from the bottle and took the snuffbox out of her lap. They lifted her onto the bed but it was too late for they couldn't straighten her legs.

Our little brother William, whose face is framed by curls like a dirt-streaked angel, has eyes bright with fever and knowing. I want him to stay but he passes too quickly. There is Charlie who was twenty when they speared him while he looked after someone else's sheep. They all died not long after you left. Father wouldn't let me go to their funerals because of what had happened. Then he died too.

Much later Jem took a black woman and they had a child. It was many years before Jem forgot. And then one day he came to my house. He never said much and there was the sweet smell of liquor that followed him. Sometimes he didn't have any money. Then he began to work for my husband who had land and sheep at Tackalarup. But George has sold them now and Jem is buried on the side of the hill that faces away from the sea.

Middle Island 1835, Dorothea Newell

Dorothea closed her eyes and turned her head away from the smoke. When her gaze returned to the fire, the smoke had lifted and in the embers she saw a house with walls of grey stone and windows that glowed and inside it was painfully blue with heat. She had been watching Anderson threaten Manning and her brother. Something about stolen money: she couldn't quite hear what was being said. It didn't surprise her. They would often find Jem where there was trouble. It was the other reason her father had sent him away to Hampshire when he was eight years of age. She did worry for him but it was a feeling she could easily reason herself out of. Particularly now that he was always with that James Manning. Manning made her uneasy for it was as though there was something that seethed beneath his skin, waiting to burst out.

~

Jansen was on the other side of the fire and the flames looked as though they were lapping his chin. He ripped chunks of meat from a bone with his teeth. When he turned to talk to the man beside him, his mouth glistened with fat. She decided that they ate better on the island than they had ever done at home.

The noise of the black women broke into her thoughts. Their voices rising and falling as they moved about in front of their fire. She never looked directly at their nakedness but under the cover of darkness her eyes were drawn to them. Their skin shone in the flickering light and their empty breasts swung unfettered. Strands of shells were wrapped in layers around their necks. Hanging from Dinah's necklace was a bone like a small jawbone which glowed against her skin.

She realised it was only Dinah and Sal who were singing.

Mooney sat quietly to one side. The other two were different. They shaved their hair and their features were finer. Mooney's face was broader, her nose and lips more pronounced, and instead of shells she wore an amulet of skin and hair. Their scars were different too. Mooney's were symmetrical lines connecting her breasts. The others had marks drawn indiscriminately on their backs and arms as well as on their chests. She never took much notice of the natives at the Sound. And it had never occurred to her to think about the women on the island. Tonight, though, she wondered where they had come from. Where were their families: their mothers and fathers, sisters and brothers and, perhaps, their children?

She looked around for her sister and straightened her legs for they had gone to sleep. Mary no longer bothered to tie her hair back and a streak of dirt smudged her cheek. Her eyes were shadowed. Matthew moved from his wife's side to Jansen's. Dorothea hadn't told Mary of Jansen's plans. There was no point. Mary noticed her and moved closer.

'Those buggers are up to something,' she said, nodding towards her husband and Jansen.

Dorothea frowned. After a while Matthew stood up and brushed the dirt from his trousers. He walked around the ring of the fire, behind the backs of the others, until he met Anderson at the doorway to the hut. When Anderson spoke his teeth flashed white but the rest of his body merged with the darkness. She sensed he was looking in their direction. She adjusted the skin that lay around her shoulders over her thin shawl. Her hands were sticky with grease and sand stuck to them. She tried to wipe it off on her gown but they just collected more dirt. She jumped as she felt a hand on her shoulder, and then looked up.

'What do you want?'

She hadn't seen Jansen get up and come around the other side of the fire. He coughed and leant down towards her.

'Get up,' he said.

'No.'

His hand was on her shoulder and he pinched her bone between his thumb and forefinger. She realised that it was useless to fight. And she didn't know what would happen if she drew attention to herself. Maybe someone would stop him but then they all might decide to take a turn. She pushed herself up off the ground. She felt sick and saliva flooded her mouth as though she was going to throw up. But she didn't.

He placed a heavy hand on her arm and led her away. As she walked beside him she thought at least if he reached the Sound he might send someone for them. She smelt the tart tang of the bush and felt the crunching beneath her feet of its dried and twisted twigs. He took her down to the beach where a sharp splinter of a moon hung before them. It was too hard to see where the sky met the sea and if she stared long enough she started to doubt that she could see anything at all. She stumbled in the sand and they moved awkwardly together. He pushed her down and it was cold on her back. The sound of the sea swamped the noise of his breathing. He lifted her skirts. She pulled them further up over her face, feeling the heat on her cheeks as she breathed against the stiff fabric. Cocooned beneath her skirts, she was reminded of her brother William who would cover his eyes and think that because he couldn't see her she was no longer there.

⁓

The canvas slapping in the wind woke her. She sat up and realised that she and Mary were alone. Mary was already awake. She didn't seem to notice Dorothea.

'Are you alright?'

She didn't answer.

Dorothea pulled herself up. Through the gap, silver light glittered on the water as it caught the wind ripples, and the sound of the waves slapping the sand suggested that the swell had risen overnight. Mary looked sideways at her.

'Matthew's gone.'

'Oh.'

She hitched up her skirts and crawled across to the entrance to look out, squinting at the brightness of the white sand beach. The whaleboat was gone. Despite Mary's distress she was relieved.

'That's good, ain't it? He can send someone for us.'

Mary's eyes were dark. She turned her head towards the dirty canvas wall.

'Anderson gave him three quid.' She paused for a moment and then continued. 'For a gown, he said.'

Dorothea frowned. Neither of them spoke for a minute. Finally she said: 'I don't understand.'

Mary brought her hand up to her forehead and covered her eyes.

'Three quid. I'm to be nice to him, he said.'

'What? Anderson?'

She nodded and choked. Dorothea reached for her arm and stroked it, thinking she always knew Matthew was a stupid bastard but she never thought he was capable of that. She didn't know what to say. She wondered why he needed three pounds, unless that sly dog Jansen was charging him for a place on the boat. But then Anderson couldn't have known that was what Matthew wanted the money for otherwise he would have stopped them from leaving.

The tent rustled behind her. At first she thought it was the wind but then she saw Mary's face. She turned around. Matthew's head was inside the tent.

'You ain't gone!' Mary mumbled and sat up, her cheeks wet.

He looked grim. His eyes flicked from her face to the ground and he moved inside.

'Bastards left without me.'

'That's alright then. You can give Anderson back his money,' said Dorothea, glaring at him.

He squatted down and reached for Mary's hand.

'It ain't like that.'

'What do you mean?' asked Dorothea while Mary gazed at him, eyes full and glassy.

He cleared his throat.

'I ain't got it.'

'What?'

'It was for me passage.'

'Does Anderson know?'

Mary's expression hadn't changed. It was like she didn't understand what he was saying. Matthew took his hand away from her.

'Yeah.'

'And?' asked Dorothea.

He shook his head and brought his hand up to his forehead, rubbing his brow.

'Why?' continued Dorothea.

He started to say something and then he paused, knowing that he had no explanation at all. Only that he had wanted so desperately to get away. The uncertainty of it all, of what might happen to him. Dorothea's jaw was tight with rage. That he was prepared to sell his own wife, the bastard! Mary, who had been sitting dumbly beside Dorothea, suddenly leapt up and flung herself at him. He fell back. A noise erupted from her, violent and torn, and her head shook. Dorothea was motionless. Matthew tried to hold Mary's wrists as she clawed him. Eventually she slumped sobbing on top of him. He pushed her off and got up, and without looking back, left the tent.

Mary curled herself tightly on her side. Her eyes were closed and dark strands of slimy hair entwined her neck. She brought her fists up under her chin and hiccuped. Dorothea reached down and gently pushed her onto her back, straightening her arms and placing them by her side. She brushed her hair away and took a piece of clean rag from between her breasts to wipe her sister's face. She talked softly about things that didn't matter. But when she suggested that she get up, Mary turned away. So eventually she left her.

Dorothea heard someone outside the hut. She moved to the doorway to see who it was. Anderson was bent over a bucket of water. She waited for him to see her. He looked up, and his eyes stayed on her face as he turned around and brought the knife up to a piece of rag. He slowly wiped the blade.

'What do you want?'

She gripped the doorway and the splinters pricked her hand. She took a deep breath and stepped outside, holding her skirt with one hand and shading her eyes from the sun with the other.

'My sister,' she began. He replaced the knife in his belt. She let her hand drop from her forehead and turned away.

'My sister,' she said more loudly, 'is married.'

Anderson grunted. She felt the heat in her face.

'You can't have her.'

He looked down at the cloth in his hand, then he wiped his arm, which was covered in sand, and grinned.

'It was her husband's idea,' he said mildly.

'But you can't keep him to it.'

He shrugged and turned away, taking the track back to the beach. She watched his back as it disappeared between the trees and then she gripped her skirts with both hands and hurried after him. His long strides put distance between them quite quickly. She called after him as they neared the headland.

'I want to know what you're going to do.'

Without running she was finding it difficult to keep up with him. He stopped.

His expression had hardened and he said: 'A dog doesn't bark at his master.'

Then he continued. Her pace slowed. She had no idea what he was talking about. She came to the seaweed beach and struggled through the mounds to the other side. It reminded her of a dream she sometimes had that no matter how hard she tried she couldn't get to the end of the road and her feet would sink further and further into deep mud.

She reached the whaleboat a few minutes after Anderson. At the same time Manning and Jem appeared from the other direction. She hadn't seen them since the evening before. She was reminded again of how little she knew her brother. He hadn't even acknowledged her. Mead and Isaac scraped the keel of the overturned boat and briefly looked up at them all. Anderson stirred a pot that simmered on a smouldering fire. It smelt of burnt toffee and its thick crimson liquid bubbled.

Isaac grinned while he worked. 'Can't get rid of you then,' he said to Manning.

Manning reached for his throat.

'We saw a sail,' he said.

'Over the other side,' added Jem, pointing towards Goose Island.

Anderson poured what looked like blood into the liquid and stirred some more.

'Was it Jansen?' asked Manning.

Mead and Isaac looked up at the boys and then over at Anderson. Mead nodded.

'Who was with him?' asked Manning, glancing warily at Anderson.

Anderson leant over the boat and with his knife wedged the resin into its joins. He didn't appear to be listening.

'There were seven of them,' replied Mead. 'Jansen's mob and that mad bastard Johno. The boy too. He's gone. Bugger me, why they took him.'

'What about Owens?' asked Manning quickly, his eyes shifting from one person to the next.

'He's gone,' said Mead slowly, watching him.

Manning shifted his weight from one foot to the other. He seemed to be studying the ground. His long thin hair covering his eyes. Then he looked up. All of them except Anderson were watching him. Then Anderson looked up too and some of the boiling liquid dropped onto his palm. He didn't flinch.

'What do you want?' asked Anderson.

'Me and him.' Manning took a deep breath and nodded at Jem. 'We want you to take us to the mainland.'

Anderson straightened. He wiped the back of his hand on the rag around his forehead but he didn't say anything. He didn't need to. In his hand the red liquid on the end of the stick hardened to a thick glassy substance. Manning looked over his shoulder at Jem and together they walked away, following the wet line of the tide. Jem stopped to look at something washed up by the sea. Manning reached down. But as he did so Dorothea caught the desperate look he gave Anderson.

She was going to speak to Anderson again but she sensed Isaac watching her. The look on his face made her skin prickle for he had eyes like the wild dogs that came in for scraps around the Sound. He scared her more than most men. She turned around and followed her brother and his friend along the beach.

'What were you talking about?' she asked Jem as she caught up with him.

He looked sideways and then across at Manning.

'Nothing.'

Why couldn't he act like her brother, just once?

'You would tell us if you were going to leave?' she continued.

This time Manning answered, and he sneered as he spoke: 'Why would he tell you anything?'

She looked at him, wondering why he was so hostile towards her. She noticed her boots were collecting sand in the holes at the toes. She stopped to sit on a rock to take them off. Manning was standing over her. She recognised his expression.

'Bugger off, you little bastard,' she spat, sickened, feeling almost as though she had been propositioned by her brother.

Manning's slippery look vanished and he walked on. She didn't try to catch up with them.

She felt sick, apprehensive sick like when they set sail from the Sound. Jansen had gone. And even though she had wanted to be free of him, his leaving made her feel more isolated than ever. She had been left behind on an island with sealers, men who had their own rules. She felt as though she was on the edge of the world, or perhaps she had fallen off into some halfway place. It wasn't living and it wasn't quite hell. She could feel the wind changing. The sea between Flinders Peak and Goose Island was ruffled with wind gusts and white-capped waves. And in the same direction a solid band of black clouds had formed and was spreading. Manning and her brother continued on past the camp to the other end of the beach where she could see Matthew. He was probably trying to trap fish on the reef. She hoped her sister wasn't in the camp for she couldn't face her.

⁓

A blackened log smoked in the fireplace and threatened to go out. She gathered some dry leaves and sticks and tried to poke it into life. Small flames wavered and smouldered and smoke filled the room. She gave up and let the smoke sting her eyes into tears. She couldn't even get a fire started. There wasn't anything she could do and she was tired of feeling responsible for everyone. It had always been like that. She had nursed her mother and tended to her cuts and bruises and made sure that all the children were fed. Mary had helped sometimes but only when she was asked to. Dorothea knew she was beaten. She had always felt she could take care of her sister. Together they were stronger than if they acted alone. It had changed of course when Mary was married, but it hadn't stopped Dorothea from wanting to try. Perhaps it was her fault that Mary was the way she was. Her sister was not unlike the short-beaded weed that grew beneath the waterline on the rock: swept one way and then another by the tide, never to stand straight.

She knew Mary was distraught. She hated Matthew for that. She knew that being married had to be marginally better than being single. But how foolish women were to believe they were protected. There was no security, ever.

She moved away from the smoke into the damp dark recesses of the room. The walls huddled around and thin pieces of stringy-bark hung drably from timber posts. She ran her hand over the table's rough surface and heard the rustling of a small creature in the eaves. Leaves and sticks scratched the roof as the wind pushed them back and forth. Looking around she noticed the half-empty barrel of black-strap stowed in the corner.

The top was firmly fastened. She found a knife and levered it off. She dipped her cup and covered the bottom. Just for a taste. She leant against the wall and stretched her legs out in front of her. Nestled in the dark corner behind the table, she was hidden from anyone entering. The fire burnt weakly and produced purple clouds that hung in the middle of the room. They tumbled about, turning this way and that and drifting up towards the roof. Dusty spiders' webs hung like clotted pieces of silver from beams and were bunched into corners. Her backside was cold and numb but then after a while she wasn't sure where the ground ended and her body began. Feet came in and out of the hut. Some stayed for a while, resting under the table. A pair of boots grinned where the soles were falling away. They were battered and scuffed. And there were feet that were black with soil and sores. She knew at the time whose they were but now she couldn't remember. Someone giggled and she smiled too. Then she opened her eyes. The black women were above her.

She could hardly see them for the fire had gone out. But she held up the cup that had been refilled more times than she could remember and muttered for them to sit down. Dinah took it from her. She dipped the cup into the keg and settled beside Dorothea. The others sat down and they passed the cup around. Dorothea nodded enthusiastically. Shy smiles flashed white like the bone around Dinah's neck. Dinah and Sal spoke to each other in their own language. Mooney handed her the cup. She drank some more. Dorothea said something. Dinah answered in English and although Dorothea wasn't sure what she said, it didn't matter. They all grinned. Time swelled and contracted. She basked in the warmth of their eyes and the grog wound its way round her body.

A woman's wail broke into her soft-edged thoughts and sharpened their focus. She was surprised they were still there. Not that she could see them for it was dark, but she sensed them. She couldn't stop her hands from shaking. She was cold and everything felt strange. She couldn't move. Whatever it was that they were doing, it resonated through her body. The sounds and the rhythm of their music combined to become a thread of sorrow that wound around them and wove them together.

She cried for their helplessness. But their broken voices continued their story and then, without warning, they stopped and she heard footsteps and men's voices. Dread loomed large like a bad spirit. She had to get up. But it was too late. Anderson was standing over them. He drew one of them up and threw her over the table. The women stayed silent. Dorothea was pulled by her hair and held against the wall. The hand around her neck was rough and tight. She saw over his shoulder in the flickering light the shadows of the women on the wall as they got up from the floor and slipped into the darkness. She also saw her brother keep his face to the fire as he fed it with more wood.

The firelight caught one eye and it was hard and cruel. The other was in shadow. Her consciousness retreated to a dark corner and it was as though she was peeking through a crack in the door at something that didn't involve her. There was no fear only vague curiosity as to what would happen next. Her arms were limp by her side. She heard him but it was a voice from a distance, then his hand left her neck and she was flung across the room. She almost fell but he was behind her again and he pulled her into the other room where she fell into a pile of skins. She lay still. But there was no movement behind her. She inhaled the deep musky scent of the fur and moved her face against its softness. So soft like silk, turning her head to look into the semi-darkness, but he had gone. She didn't move but then the fight had left her anyway.

~

Sometime later but she wasn't sure how much later a triangle of yellow light passed across the wall. Anderson held the lamp out in front of him and black animals prowled the room. She was lying on her side. Out of the corner of her eye she saw him move across the room and set the lamp down and then the animals were still. She curled herself into a tighter curve. He was standing at her feet.

'Think I prefer you anyway.'

She closed her eyes.

'Or maybe I'll have you both.' He chuckled to himself.

'No!'

Her head swung around and she looked up at him, wide-eyed. He started to unbutton his trousers but then he stopped. He knelt down and pulled her legs so that she was lying on her back.

'Take off your gown.'

No one had ever asked her to take off her clothes. She wrapped her arms over her breasts and stared up into his face. It wasn't that she was scared, it was just that it was unnatural. The whites around his eyes weren't as white as she'd thought. More like yellow with a lot of spidery red lines. And his eyes, they bulged a bit and were big and round. And they were so dark that she couldn't make out the coloured bit from the black circle in the middle. They were sort of expressionless like he hated her. Just before his fist connected with her jaw she knew he was going to hit her. The side of her face burnt and her ear rang. Salty liquid seeped onto her tongue.

He wavered through the watery film in her eyes. Slowly she sat up and looked down at her feet which were bare. She edged back to the wall behind her and slid up it. He watched as though he expected her to come at him like some old klapmatch. She leant sideways against it, facing away from him, slowly reaching for her buttons. Edging her shoulder, rounded and white, from the top of the gown, the fabric peeling away like the skin from a seal, and she stood huddled and cold against the prickly timber. He came closer and pulled her wrist so that she stood facing him and he stepped back, eyes narrowed and breathing louder. She watched the insects flying into the lamp. He came towards her again and placed a hand on her breast. She looked down as it covered the rounded mound of her skin. His touch was hot and almost gentle but the rest of it wasn't. Crushed by his weight, the wet salt of his sweat and the rank odour of his breath, she lay without moving beneath him. When he rolled off, the cold air seared her raw skin.

'Get out,' he said.

She fumbled for her gown and dressed in front of him, and as she left she glanced over her shoulder at his naked body. She clutched the side of the doorway as she passed into the other room, unsteady on her feet. Orange eyes winked in the hearth. She felt her way around the table and chairs to where she knew there was a pail of water. The only sound was that of her feet shuffling across the floor. Perhaps they were the only ones left. Perhaps the others were dead, or maybe they had left in Anderson's boat. Thunder rattled the rafters and she jumped. But she knew that was fanciful too. She could see plates and fish heads on the table. The wet dirt stuck to her feet. It had been raining. She had forgotten where she had left her boots. But it didn't really matter for they weren't much use any more. The bucket should be there but it wasn't. She bent over and felt with her hands along the edge of the fireplace but she couldn't find it. She was so thirsty; she would die if she didn't have some water.

Outside the air was crisp and clouds rushed across the moon. It was lighter too. And the leaves glistened. The wet ground deadened the sound of her footsteps, but still as she followed the track she heard the thump, thump of the tammar as they warned one another and rustled through the undergrowth. Carefully she parted the wet branches that crossed her path and continued until she came to the well. Her feet were numb, caked with sticky mud, and the sleeves of her gown were soaked. She wasn't cold even though the water was warmer than her hands. She drank from them, sitting on the side of the well with the pail between her legs, listening to the joyous song of the frogs.

There was a sound to her right, not a normal night sound. She dared not swallow. Her pulse pumped as though her heart would jump right out of her chest. Straining her eyes to form shapes in the blackness. Something radiated warmth and smelt of charcoal. And then the clouds thinned over the moon and its light caught the bone around her neck which rose and fell on her chest as she breathed.

'It's you,' Dorothea murmured.

Dinah didn't answer but moved closer. Dorothea was relieved it wasn't Isaac or any of the others, but then she was uneasy. Dinah held out her hand as though she wanted to give her something. Dorothea looked at it for a moment and then held out her own and felt Dinah place in it something smooth and hard. It was a bone strung from plant fibre, like the one Dinah wore. Dorothea turned it over and looked up but Dinah had gone. Even though it sat neatly in the cradle of her palm, she felt repulsed by it. But when she touched it with her thumb she was comforted by its smooth luminous surface.

She carried water back to the hut and washed by the coals that still gave off some warmth. Then she went into the storeroom and lay on the pile of skins in the corner.

A bird warbled as though dawn was close but it didn't feel as though she had slept. But she must have. Her head ached and she heard Anderson moving around in the other room. His footsteps went into the kitchen and when she stood in the doorway he was shovelling ash from the hearth and replacing it with a mess of firewood. He bent over, bare to the waist, blowing clouds of ash as he coaxed the spark into a flame. He sensed her behind him and he moved quickly to face her.

'Don't stand behind me.'

Dorothea came across the room to the fire. His eyes followed her. She stared into the fireplace. He reached over and turned her face towards him. Lightly he touched the bruise on her cheek and when she looked into his face she was surprised by what she saw. And then he left the room. And she was uncertain whether she had really seen what looked like regret.

She wrapped her arms around herself and rubbed them, watching the flames as they leapt into life. Light steps padded across the floor. She knew without looking that it was her sister. Mary clasped her shawl tightly and shook with cold.

'Here, come closer.' Dorothea grasped her arm and led her to the fire. 'How come you're wet?'

'Rain blew into the tent,' she shivered.

Dorothea rubbed her back. Anderson walked in with an armful of firewood and they stepped back as he set it down. Soon the fire was bursting with heat and they seared their hands in front of it.

'Jack,' she started. Their eyes met and then she continued. 'We'd be more comfortable here than in that leaking tent.'

He nodded. Dorothea turned back to the fire and smiled to herself.

'There ain't nothing to worry about,' she said quietly to Mary.

January 1886

Children used to come to the side door of this house to buy sweets and boiled lollies. They were happy sounds. Now there is silence. Sometimes I hear the steps of people passing along the lane to the houses at the back. There is George walking below. Stoking the fire and settling into the chair that was mine. It is beside the fireplace facing the front window. From there you can see the new jetty and the entrance to the Sound. I used to watch the steamers belch black smoke as they rumbled into the harbour past Possession Point, so different from the fine lines of the sailing ships.

If he were to turn the chair so that he was looking straight ahead, he would face Big Grove across the harbour. That was where our father died. Burning lime. He and Jem bought land there after they sold the house on the hill. They would bring lime and timber across the water to the landing stage, which lay on the shore to the right of this house. I used to watch them steady the flat-bottomed boat that lay deep in the water. Once they had unloaded onto the dray and taken their money, they would walk across to the inn.

Through the doorway the grey light brightened. Isaac leant against the wooden frame and drew on his pipe. Smoke leaked from his nose and out the corners of his mouth.

Mead looked up from the strands of grass he was twisting together on the table.

'Are we taking her out?'

Isaac shook his head and glanced behind him.

'There's more weather coming.'

At the other end of the table Manning flicked the wooden chips, displaying the spots he had carved onto the surfaces. He picked them up again and held them between his fingers and then released them onto the table letting them clatter across it. Everyone looked up. He smirked. Church leant over the table and picked one up, turning it over.

'Here, leave it!' Manning snatched it back.

Church shrugged and left it on the table. Dorothea knew Manning irritated everyone.

'What's wrong with you?' she asked, standing over him, knowing that he hated it when she looked down at him.

She wanted to annoy him. There was nothing he could do to her, although she knew he liked to think there was. His eyes narrowed and he gathered up the dominoes in a piece of leather and wrapped twine around the top. It was almost a week since they had been trapped inside because of the weather. Hail had broken through the roof and wind bent the trees back.

Mead coiled the twine and then began to sharpen his knife, rubbing it slowly across a round grey stone and occasionally spitting on it. She placed a cup of tea beside him but he didn't look up as he moved the knife in careful circles. Hair grew out of his face, coarse and sparse, and the skin beneath it was raw. His eyes were blue as the sea on a clear day and enveloped in folds of scaly skin that creased in the corners. He laid down the knife and took the cup with both hands.

Isaac left the doorway. She put down the other cup. She felt his eyes on her but she had grown used to it. She went back to the fire and filled more cups. She gave one to Matthew but as usual he ignored her. Church thanked her as he wrote on a piece of bark.

She joined Mary at the fire and they drank their tea listening to the wind moan into the corners and whip the trees so that the branches scraped across the roof of the hut.

'Where's our tea then?'

Dorothea looked over her shoulder at Manning and Jem.

'Make it yourself.'

She put her legs up on the stone ledge in front of her, warming her feet alongside Mary's. Manning was always angry and it had fuelled her brother's resentment.

<hr>

Anderson filled the entrance, wet and sleek, one hand around the neck of a big grey bird and the other around his gun. His mouth set like stone. Eyes swept the room. He dropped everything by the door and took off the skin cloak, flicking water from it. The fire hissed. His pale palms faced the coals and then he turned to warm his back.

'Where'd you get it?' asked Isaac.

'Over the back. Nesting.'

Isaac's chair scraped the floor. He lifted the bird by its thick red legs and looked closely at the grey and brown feathers that were speckled towards the tail.

'Good size and all.'

'Went for me, the ornery bastard. There were eggs but I couldn't carry them.'

Looking at the bird but looking at Anderson, seeing the chest and the curve of his arm and the black bush winking between them. Isaac held out the goose towards her.

'Here woman.'

Anderson turned and acknowledged her. The bird's feathers were the same colour as her gown. Mary lifted the pot of water onto the hook above the fire. When it had boiled Dorothea thrust the goose into it and then tied its legs with rope and hung it from a hook in the beam. It swung, wings outstretched, water dripping down the end of its black and yellow beak. And she stripped it: a pile of down pooling around her feet, wet feather smells and her hands itching from the wispy bits that clung to them.

They roasted the big-breasted bird over a nest of coals and fat drizzled into the fire, sizzling and smelling of a rich man's house. The other women brought in their wooden troughs filled with dirt-covered bulbs and roots and grubs that moved. Green potatoes were dug up from the garden at the back. And when everything was cooked, the fare was laid out on the table like the feast she had served for her employer at the Sound. They sat around the table, Anderson at the head, his back to the fire. But they ate with their fingers and the knives used for skinning and not with the silver she had helped Mrs McLeod unpack from the crates that came from England.

Anderson glanced at Isaac. 'We'll put the boat in the water.'

Isaac didn't say anything.

'Needs to be settled for a bit,' he said. 'And the wind's dropping off.'

Isaac nodded. Mary reached across for another potato. Dorothea was glad she was eating more. Her sister's cheeks were flushed and her eyes sparkled but it wasn't the feverish look of a few days ago. Her hair was like the matted sponge they found on the beach.

When Mary had found out Dorothea had known Jansen was leaving, she hadn't been angry. Instead she had cried quietly for most of the day, grieving for her family who she felt were even further away than ever. But in the evening her eyes, although red, were brighter and she and Dorothea laughed together when Church offered to teach them their letters. They were looking at his brown-inked writing. Dorothea asked what he was doing. He frowned and pointed the quill into his cheek.

His eyes stared unfocused for a moment and then he said: 'I am trying to remember Pope's "Ode on Solitude" but all I can remember is the last verse.'

Mary started to say something but Dorothea interrupted: 'Tell me, how does it go?'

He held out the piece of bark. When he realised her eyes were still on his face, he cleared his throat and read:

Thus let me live, unseen, unknown;
Thus unlamented let me dye;
Steal from the world and not a stone
Tell where I lye.

She shuddered as cold air brushed the back of her neck.
'So what else are you writing?'
Church shrugged.
'I'm keeping a diary.'
'What for?'
'Because if I don't, I might never have lived.'
'That's a bit sad, ain't it?' she said lightly, a smile in her voice.

'Can you write?' he asked, not hearing her.

'What?'

'Do you know your letters?'

Dorothea nodded but it was tentative. Mary looked away at a broken cobweb hanging in a single strand from the ceiling. They had missed it earlier.

'I can teach you.'

And that was when they laughed, probably more loudly than they should have. Church blinked slowly and a screen came down over his earnest eyes.

⌒

They ate without speaking. Manning and Jem's silences were heavy with unspoken words. They exchanged looks. Mary did not talk to Matthew. She was ignoring him and had been sleeping with her sister in the storeroom. But it was Anderson's actions that Dorothea found puzzling. He knew they had taken shelter in his hut but he hadn't tried to take her again. She was relieved. But as the days passed she became more aware of him. Matthew wiped his knife on his trouser leg and returned it to its sheath. She wondered if he was still sleeping in the tent or under the verandah with the men.

Wood sparked and spat in the fireplace and a thin layer of smoke hung over their heads. She and her sister had discovered that the timber inland provided more heat and burnt longer than the twisted trunks of trees that grew closer to the beach. The hut was cleaner too. They had swept out the hearth and raked the floor and reached up into the corners for spiders. The table had been moved and they had brought an empty chest from the storeroom for the clean cups and plates. More hooks hung cooking pots. It could have been their home at the Sound when their mother hadn't been drinking. It was only the skins hanging from the walls to keep out the draught that made it look any different.

Isaac relit his pipe. His fat blackened knuckles pushed the long thin stem into the parting of hair that was his mouth. His eyes narrowed as he let the smoke seep through whiskers stained brown by tobacco. Mead pushed his chair back and lit his pipe too. He clasped the bowl of the pipe in the palm of his hand. The other end he placed in the corner of his mouth and puffed from the side as it caught alight. The smell reached over her like the soft comforting touch of a baby's blanket.

When she was small and cradled by the hard warm arms of her father the smell of rum and tobacco on his breath and in his clothes enclosed her and kept her safe. She was surprised she remembered. For that feeling of security she had felt in her father's arms hadn't lasted for long. Their father had lost interest in his children when there were more than three of them. The more children, the more he was reminded of his failure to provide. He had married his boss's daughter because Dorothea's grandfather had lost his farm to the creditors and he couldn't pay his workmen. It was after Napoleon had surrendered and corn prices had fallen, terribly.

Dorothea's mother wasn't prepared for labouring life. She followed her husband to a farm in Hampshire where they worked and were given a cottage to live in. Dorothea remembered that when her father came home at the end of the week smelling of grog and the pipe, instead of gathering up his children in his arms, he would silently stand over their mother and watch her exhausted attempts to finish the washing, which he thought should have been done on Monday.

After William was born, her father lost his job. They returned to the village in Surrey where Dorothea's grandmother was living alone, relying on handouts from the parish. Their father became an itinerant labourer, following the harvest: hay-making near London and then back to Surrey for the corn harvesting later in the year. Dorothea remembered her grand-mother looking after the little ones while the rest of them worked in the fields, tying up the sheaves of corn. She saw then her dear papery face, powdered in patches for her eyesight was going, and heard her sweet low voice that never admonished anyone.

Anderson finished eating and folded his arms behind his head.

'Whales over the back.'

Dorothea looked up.

'Where?' she asked, and when he turned she realised he had been talking to Mead and Isaac. But he answered.

'Just below the cliffs. Two adults.'

'It's been a while since we seen a whaler,' said Mead.

Isaac nodded and spouted smoke from his nostrils like the dragon of her grandmother's stories.

'That was dirty, stinking work,' continued Mead.

'Wouldn't know,' said Isaac.

'You was on a whaler, Jack?'

Anderson nodded but his eyes looked beyond Mead's head.

'You know I can still remember what we had to eat,' said Mead. 'Monday, corn, beans and pork. Tuesday was codfish and beef; Wednesday, mush and beef; Thursday, corn, beans and pork …'

'How interesting,' muttered Isaac.

Anderson's eyes finally focused on Mead.

'That were an Englishman's whaler,' he said and pushed his chair back and stood up.

He turned his attention to Manning and Jem.

'Come on, we're putting the boat in.'

Manning looked as though he was about to say something. Dorothea couldn't see Anderson's face but his expression must have stopped him for Manning quietly got up from the table, followed by Jem. And then they all left except Church.

That was the other thing that puzzled Dorothea. Anderson left Church alone. He never told him to do anything. Church was a shadowy figure in a long ragged coat who hovered on the edge of their circle. Often she forgot he was there. She wondered what he wrote in his diary. She was the only one in her family who could write her name and that was because she was her grandmother's favourite. She ran her hands along the rough edge of the table and remembered that her grandmother's hands had been fine and soft. Her mother's hands must have been like that before she married their father. Grandmother would scrub her palms and her fingernails and after she had wiped them dry with a cloth, starched white with pretty pink flowers sewn into the corners, she would rub perfumed oil into them. It was just as well that Grandmother never knew the place they had come to.

She could see in Mary her mother's likeness. They had married weak men. But she knew they didn't have a choice. Both women were a burden to their families. Dorothea knew that her father would marry them all off if he could, even the younger ones. It was another reason why she had left for Van Diemen's Land. She wanted a choice. She wanted a strong man who would protect her from other men. When the image of Anderson appeared and she remembered the heat of his hand on her skin, she quickly banished it, for he didn't count.

⁓

She wrapped her shawl like a scarf over her head and tied the skin around her shoulders. Damp sand stuck to her feet.

The other end of the beach was shrouded in fine mist. The sea was black and fierce and its thick white edge washed the shore. Further out, where the swell rolled unbroken from the south, blistered by the wind, foam peaks formed and fell and were a jagged edge along the horizon. A mass of wet clouds tumbled above the waves and then a grey veil crossed the sea. Light leaked through the cracks and the mainland came and went. She breathed the damp air and pushed back her shawl, letting her hair free. The end of the beach came closer. Thick cloud crossed to the islands in the east. Above the sky lightened and the seaweed, gold and brown, shone in piles on shimmering sand. She wandered amongst them, a ragged grey figure, moving the wet silky strands aside with her toe, searching for signs of another world.

Occasionally she knelt down to look at a shell or a piece of sponge or some strange opaque creature. Animal or plant, she wasn't sure. On her way back she walked closer to the waves, and they swirled warmly around her ankles. A piece of brown rubbery weed was being nudged further up the beach by the foam. But it wasn't weed. Carefully she lifted it with both hands. Its eyes were only just still. It had a long nose, flared at the end, and its neck curved like a jaunty pony; its body was almost translucent and flowed into a tail that curled. Skin ribbed and ribbons of weed. It was a sea dragon.

The bow of the boat nudged around the point. She felt for the sea dragon to make sure it hadn't fallen from the shawl she had knotted behind her neck. She wasn't sure why she kept it. She didn't want it to smell like the large shell she and Mary had found washed up a few days ago. She walked from the wet sand onto the gently sloping rock, feet numb from the cold, trying to avoid the sharp broken shells that were dropped from the sky by the big black and white gulls. Water had pooled in small depressions in the rock. She also avoided the black patches of granite in case they were slippery. There in the corner of the bay the wind was still. But further out the tops of the waves were white and irregular. She sat on a section of dry rock and leant up against one of the boulders that were arranged like the pebbles of a giant. The boat was rowed closer to shore. The sail was wound around the mast and brought down. It lay beside each man and poked out over the stern. Anderson stood above them, head cocked to the shore, one leg raised against the leeward side, the long steering oar an extension of his arm as he manoeuvred them clear of the rocks. She thought it usually sat higher in the water but then she realised they had taken down the washcloths, the strips of canvas that were strung above the gunwales. It looked leaner and sleek and with each stroke moved cleanly through the water. When they nosed it up on the sand, the wind muffled Anderson's words. She watched him though. He leapt over the side into waist-high water. His chest sucked in with the shock of it, his arms were held above his head. He ran his hand along the side of the boat, tracing the elegant curve of the empty vessel, and then stood back from the men as they lifted it forwards onto the first roller.

They hauled it above the high-tide mark and gently set it down on the sand tilted to one side. The men left for the camp. Anderson returned with a pail. Her steps were light on the sand so that he only saw her when she gripped the side of the boat beside him. He sprang back angry.

'What are you doing?' he snapped.

She was startled.

'What?'

'Coming up on me like that. Could've knifed you.' And then he leant over and with one finger traced a line under her neck. 'Across here.'

But his look on that bare section of skin beneath her chin was soft. Despite her coverings she shivered. He turned back to the boat but not before she thought she saw the briefest of smiles. It was hard to tell for he always recovered his mask so quickly. But she had seen more than once that his eyes didn't always belong in that hard face. Still, she didn't doubt that he could be cruel. She only just reached the top of his shoulder. Despite the weather his arms were bare. He leant down to take out the rest of the water swirling around the bottom.

'Is it leaking?'

'Perhaps.' He turned his head to the side to face her as he leant over the boat. 'Stupid bastards hauled her up without taking out the water.'

He straightened and threw out the contents of the pail.

'Been out of the sea too long. The timber shrinks.'

She nodded and looked down the line of the boat and the neat rows of planking at the bottom and remembered what it had been like to sail here. They were long thin boats and on each seat, or thwart as the men called them, one man took an oar. The only place she and her sister could sit was up the front beside the mast. And the waves had been so big. When the boat plunged into the trough, she and her sister clutched the sides, expecting the bow to part the thick blue walls and take them beyond the darkness. But while the front of the boat might sink a little and their faces become wet with the spray, it would rise up and totter above the next wave, only to begin again.

She took her hand away from the boat, suddenly reminded of what lay between her and the place she had come from.

'What do you want?' he asked.

She half turned and shrugged. With the movement of her shoulders she noticed the creature hanging in the folds of her shawl. She took it out and he took it from her, turning it over and holding it close to his face.

'Have you seen one before?'

He nodded. 'They're good luck.'

She looked sceptical and he chuckled and the sound sort of rumbled in his chest.

'At Wampoa the Chinamen had big baskets full. They were dried for eating I think. They ate all crazy things those Chinamen.' He gave it back to her. 'But he don't look too tasty.'

That's what she would do. She would dry it.

⁓

Mary was beside the door to the kitchen. When she saw Dorothea her breath burst from her chest.

'There you are. Thank God.'

'What's wrong?'

''Twas a woman screaming. I thought it was you.'

'Where?'

'Round the back.'

Her sister grabbed the back of her skirt.

'What are you doing?'

Dorothea paused, listening. She couldn't hear anything. But then there was something that came through faintly over the top of the thundering sea. Like an animal whimpering. She continued along the track. When she reached the well she saw her. She wasn't sure who it was until she came closer. It was Mooney, bleeding from the side of her head. She was tethered to the tree by the well. The eye without blood glanced up and away, almost ashamed.

Dorothea felt for the thin trunk of the tree beside her and wrapped her hand around its flaky surface. She wanted to go closer but her legs wouldn't move. Then from behind a tree came Isaac. He had a club in his hand and as he passed Mooney he raised it above his head as though to hit her again. When she sank into the dirt he laughed and brought his hand down by his side. He walked towards Dorothea and then he saw her.

'Fancy a bit too?'

'You can't do that to her. It's not right.'

'I do what I bleedin' like.'

He was too close for her to run and his face was in her face and the inside of his mouth was like a wet black cavern. His cold eyes bulged. She gasped with the stench of his breath as he spat.

'Here, I'll give you what you want.'

She turned her head away and he grabbed her hair, holding it tight against her skull. Her eyes watered. His other hand he thrust under her skirt and his fingers invaded her and he laughed in her face.

'This is it … ain't it … this what you been wanting.'

She struggled against him, pushing his chest with her hands, but he didn't budge. Instead he was pushing her backwards into the bush. She was going to fall. He let go as she fell into the wattle, tearing the sleeves of her gown and scratching her arms. Her mind registered the startled squawk of a rock parrot and sharp pricks of the undergrowth beneath her. He stood over her undoing the buttons on his trousers.

There was a snap like the sound of a thick branch breaking and he fell sideways into the bush. She looked up and saw Anderson standing over him. Mary was behind Anderson. She took Mary's hand to pull herself up.

'Jack … Jack … the black woman. He tied her up.'

Anderson looked back at her and his eyes squinted hard.

'It's his woman.'

She sat on a chair by the fire while Mary washed the blood from the scratches on her face and arms. Her gown was ruined. The fabric was worn anyway and now the seams had split from the shoulders.

'Did you see her? Mooney?' asked Dorothea.

Mary shook her head as she dipped the rag in water.

'It ain't right,' continued Dorothea.

'And there ain't nothing you can do about it.'

'But …'

'It ain't nothing to do with us.'

Dorothea sighed and looked down at the cuts on her hands. They were only shallow wounds.

It was suddenly dark. Mary took a stick from the fire and lit the lamp in the middle of the table. Anderson came through the door with her shawl. He threw it at her and gave her a look that was blacker than his skin. She hadn't realised she had lost it. And then she remembered the sea dragon. She felt for its outline and uncovered it. But it was crushed and so she threw it onto the fire and watched it sizzle and shrink and the firelight flickered in her eyes.

She sensed his movement behind her and when he left the room she murmured to Mary that she was going to bed. Mary came too and they lay on their bed of skins in the storeroom. Neither of them slept but they felt safer listening to the men's voices through the crack under the door. Dorothea thought he would come for her but he didn't. Mary's breathing was deep and even. The light went out and then all she could hear was the scurrying of small animals and branches sliding back and forth against the outside wall whenever there was a gust of wind.

She spread the skins she was going to use out on the floor. Anderson was angry with her. She knew that much. That morning he had stood with his back to the fire, watching them all, waiting for a reason to snarl. Isaac had bristled silently in the corner and she knew he would do more than beat her if he had half a chance. She guessed that Anderson was angry because he felt he had to defend her. Perhaps he was angrier with himself. She shuddered and wondered if Isaac would try it again. Not while Anderson was in charge of the camp. But what if he wasn't? She brushed the hair from her eyes and made an effort to think of something else. The men had gone sealing, for the day was still and cloudless. They wouldn't be back for two or three days. It was just her and her sister and Church.

She looked down at the pile of skins she had brought from the storeroom. On some the hair was coarse and the leather thick and unyielding; on others the fur was soft like silk and the skin supple and light, and there were different shades of brown and gold and silver-grey. She would make a coat. As she ran her fingers over the fur, she remembered the fur-seal hat and stole she had seen for sale in a ladies salon in London. The skins from the other bundle would have been better but she couldn't use them for they were the ones that would fetch the high prices. They had white-tipped silvery guard hairs and a thick rich chestnut underfur. The ones in front of her looked moth-eaten for they had bald patches in places where the animal had been scarred, probably from the teeth of a shark or another seal. She would cut around them. Just as she brought the knife up to the leather, Mary's dirty feet appeared. She stood in the doorway. Golden light framed her head and kept her face in the dark.

'It's sunny out.'

'I can see that. Do you want any of this?'

Mary didn't say anything for a moment.

'Mmm, I suppose.'

'There's plenty. And if we're here for winter …'

'I hope not.'

Dorothea didn't reply.

Mary remained standing. 'Don't you ever think of home? Or wonder what they're doing?'

'Of course, but it would be no different.'

'I know … I was just wondering how Netty is and all.'

'She'll be alright.'

'Don't you miss them?'

Dorothea replied by hacking into the skin with the knife. She did miss William, her little brother. But she had grown tired of being mother to the others. Now it was Netty's turn. Mary bent down and picked up one of the skins. She held it out in front of her. It had holes where the flippers had been cut away.

'Don't have to do much to this.'

She put her arms through the holes and it was like a shapeless coat. She giggled as she spun around. Dorothea smiled.

'Tis the latest fashion from London,' said Mary in her best voice.

Dorothea draped another around her shoulders. She walked up and down the hut with her head turned to the side, skirts gathered high and stepping on her toes. Mary was choking with laughter. Dorothea's spirits rose in response to her sister's lightness of mood, particularly as it was so uncharacteristic. Church walked in. They stopped and looked at each other and caught their giggles. He cleared his throat and kept his eyes on the ground.

'Excuse me,' he muttered.

'Tis alright Mister Church. Please come in and make yourself comfortable,' said Dorothea, her face pink with the effort of trying not to laugh.

They gathered up the skins and took them outside where it was easier to see. They sat with their backs to the sun, squinting at the shimmering fur covering their knees, and made holes to thread the twine through. In front was the hut and above it a wispy smudge from the fire in an otherwise blemish-free sky that stretched endless and blue. A raven flapped its wings in the foliage and called sharply over the melodic twittering of little birds. And the sea breathed back and forth. Their heads bent over their work, and their hands pushing and pulling to penetrate the tough seal hides.

That evening they displayed their garments to Church. He was at the other end of the table. They had made coats with sleeves, the fur turned inwards. They were proud of their efforts. Church noticing, nodded. After a while Dorothea took off her coat, for even though the night was cold it was too hot to wear inside. It was strange with just the three of them. The night noises seemed louder than usual and even though she hadn't often noticed the black women slipping in and out of the hut, she noticed now when they didn't. She asked Church to get them some more wood. The door scraped across the floor and they listened to his footsteps as he trod on sticks that lay across the path behind the hut. Then silence dropped on them, heavy and suffocating, so that when Dorothea spoke her voice sounded strangled.

'He seems to be taking a while.'

Mary looked over at the door and back at Dorothea. Then he pushed it open and everything was alright again. They fed the fire and poked it up into a bright blaze. Shadows danced on the walls. They ate bread and a broth made from the leftover bones of the goose, which they drank from cups.

She lay on her skins, warm and well fed and yet sleep seemed distant. There was something bothering her. It was probably just the lumps and bumps in her bedding. She turned over and moved the coverings but then she woke Mary. So she got up and went into the kitchen where she relit the lamp and stared into the dying coals. Charred wallaby and goose bones lay amongst the ash. They reminded her of the bone Dinah had given her. Where had she put it? She had meant to throw it away on her way back from the well but when she had reached the hut she had realised it was still in her hand so she had put it on the shelf. Now she felt for it, her hands running along the wood. It was still there and in her palm it was iridescent. She didn't know why but she fastened it around her neck. Then she took the lamp into Anderson's room and stood at the doorway while the light wavered. When she had looked back that night he had been lying there, shiny and purple. She crept forward and placed the lamp on the chest. She sat on his skins and pulled his coverings around her and put out the light.

⁓

They were on the other side of the point beneath Flinders Peak when they saw the sail. Mary noticed it first. They had been collecting limpet shells. There was not much wind and the dark shapes bent with the oars as they moved along the sparkling sea. Dorothea squinted into the midday sun. She thought at first that it was Anderson. But she knew from the way the man stood at the steering oar that it wasn't him. Mary shielded her eyes from the glare with one hand and raised her other arm. Dorothea looked back out to sea. Then she took

Mary's arm and lowered it, stepping back towards the sandhill, bringing her with her.

'What are you doing?'

'It ain't them.'

Mary looked again. 'Are you sure?'

Dorothea nodded. The boat was nearing the point, turning to head into the bay in front of the camp. She still had hold of Mary's arm and she gripped it more tightly.

'Ouch!'

She released her hand from Mary's wrist.

'Sorry. Where's Church?'

Mary shrugged. 'I think he was in the hut.' And then she asked: 'Who do you think it is?'

'Don't know but they're sealers.'

The boat vanished into the corner of the bay.

'I don't think we should go back until they're gone.' She added quietly, 'That's if they go.'

They went inland up through soft sand and thick twisted wattle, fighting the dead foliage that crossed their path, sometimes on their hands and knees through the wallaby trails. The little animals were all around them. They would thump the ground and crash through the undergrowth but the two women never saw them. The bush enclosed them and muffled the sea. Eventually it cleared and they clambered over rock. From the highest point they could see Goose Island Bay and the pink lake. But not the corner of the bay where a boat might have been pulled up. They came down the other side and leant up against the warm steep rock that curled over them like a wave.

The sun was low in the sky when Dorothea thought about getting up. The warm rays no longer reached them and she shivered.

'I'm thirsty,' said Mary as she got up and stretched.

'There's a rock pool back there.'

'Can't we go back?'

Dorothea was standing above her, looking across to the camp. She could see a thick winding spiral of smoke.

'I don't think they've gone.'

'But ... well we can't spend the night here.'

'Might have to.'

'That's stupid ... I'm going back.'

Dorothea shook her head.

'We don't know them.'

Mary looked away, rubbing her arms. Dorothea could see the sea on three sides of the island. The setting sun lit the face of a dome-shaped island so that it reared out of the water like some strange apparition. The mainland seemed so close. The flat islands to the northeast were like stepping stones towards it. She wondered where Anderson had gone. Then she remembered he said he was going east to an island where there were fur seals. She hoped he would be back soon. It would be cold tonight. They couldn't light a fire and what would they eat? She wished she knew where the Aboriginal women found their berries and their bulbs. They had limpets. She gritted her teeth and shuddered. She couldn't eat them raw though.

They could almost see the sun sinking, it disappeared so quickly. The burning disc weaved through crimson clouds and dropped behind the land edge. And then scarlet streaks faded to purple as the sky darkened and the first star appeared above them. The spongy lichen at the base of the rock was soft and damp. They lay on one of their coats and placed the other over the top of them. Dorothea wrapped her arm across Mary's stomach to keep them close together. She closed her eyes, willing the night to be short and trying not to think what they would do if the sealers were not gone tomorrow.

'Do you remember when we was children and we got lost?'

'Mmm.'

Mary continued: 'We was playing in the field behind the church and we went into the forest and we couldn't find our way back.'

Dorothea sighed. 'I remember.'

'We lay in the bush like this until morning and they found us. And Mother she hugged us so tight I can remember I thought she was going to squeeze me in half.'

Dorothea had forgotten that bit. And then she remembered what the morning light had looked like through the trees overhead, broad leaves, soft and green and dappled and glowing, sliding over one another in the breeze. The picture was hazy and the only colour from England she could remember was green. So different from their new home which was drab and dreary. But then when the sun shone it could be startling and brilliant. A landscape of colours she had never seen before.

⁓

Mary stirred beside her. The sky was pale purple and the odd star remained. They were wet, the heavy air had left droplets on their hair and faces and the skin that covered them. Her fingers were frozen and her back and her legs were cold. She knew that if she moved she'd let in the cold air between them but if she didn't she would become stiff. They shook the moisture from their coats and put them on. They climbed back up the rock to see if there was any activity at the camp.

There was no smoke. Dorothea stood still for a moment, thinking. The island sparkled and shone and below her the tops of the trees rippled. If they were still at the camp they would have lit a fire. Perhaps it was best to return and hide in the bush near the camp so they could see what was happening.

They trod through clumps of green and brown, their feet sinking every now and then into a muttonbird burrow. The scrub began to thicken again and then it opened out into a thicket of tall trees. Cool and enclosed with a grassy floor, treetops towered above them and rustled in the breeze. Long strips of bark like shredded rags hung from the limbs of tall eucalypts. They startled a big black goanna that stiffened on splayed legs then shot into a burrow at the base of a trunk. The sea was a muffled boom and a fly whined. Discarded bark crackled beneath their feet. The sea flickered through the gaps in the trees and they knew they were heading in the right direction. Then they reached the thickets of ti-tree that lined the beach.

The wind had picked up, blowing strongly from the northwest and whipping up whitecaps out to sea. A boat was on the beach and men walked from it towards the hut.

'That's Matthew,' said Mary in surprise.

Dorothea recognised their brother too and Anderson. She picked up her skirts and looked down at her hands that were scratched and stinging. Her ankles too were spotted with blood. She turned to Mary, wondering if she looked as battered as her sister. Her face was marked by dirt and framed by hair that was knitted with twigs and leaves. Around her neck, the fur of her skin coat curled outwards. They came over the crest of the hill and almost walked into him. When Anderson saw her, his eyes widened and he grabbed her arms, tightly so that it hurt.

'Ouch … what are you doing?'

She pulled backwards but he held firm, his eyes fiercely intense. At first she thought he was going to hit her. He didn't say anything. It was as though he didn't have the words. And then he let go and walked around her to the beach. She stood rubbing her arms, wondering.

On their return they discovered the sealers had beaten Church. They bathed his wounds and listened. He told how he was tied up. He said they ransacked the camp, taking with them an unopened barrel of flour and a bundle of skins before leaving early that morning. Anderson said he knew who it was.

Later when she brought water from the well to wash their dishes, he stopped her before she reached the door. This time he took her arm gently and she let him but she turned her face towards the darkness. He didn't say anything for a moment but she could feel his eyes moving over the side of her face.

'Bastards. They always find me. They take everything. I send them to hell.'

He paused and brought his other hand up to his chest, rubbing it, and she sensed that he had turned away.

'I had no life when I came over the sea but I found another. I'm reborn … like Jesus.'

Startled, she turned. His features were loose and the moonlight caught the white of his eye. But when he turned back, he was grinning.

Then his grin disappeared and he said: 'They won't get another chance.'

There was no light after he had closed the door. He let go of her arm and she could feel with her feet that she was at the base of his bed.

'Take off your gown,' he muttered.

She didn't want to for it was cold. He was waiting for her to do something. She could feel the heat from his body even though they weren't touching. Breathing beside her. Then he moved his hands to her waist, along the seam of the fabric, until he reached under her arms and then over the swell of her breasts, tracing the outline with his fingers. She noticed the heat in her face and a sensation that came from her core and outwards, flowing fluid and loose, and contracting. Her breath caught and he moved his hands up over her shoulders, pushing back her coat, and she let it fall down her arms and onto the floor. He stepped back then and she could hear him undressing. She was out of her gown and his fingers found her again, pressing her down, hands coarse from calluses that scratched her skin so that she shivered. She breathed into his salty neck and traced the hard curves of his arms and shoulders, following the scars crossing his back as he pushed into her and she opened: soft moist skin that enclosed.

January 1886

I still wear the bone of the black woman's child around my neck. I learnt afterwards that Dinah's people wore the bones of their friends and loved ones to ward off harm and illness. She told me that it was the bone of her child. Her children were not allowed to live. After everything that happened I am glad of her gift.

I do not have anything of my daughter, not even a lock of her hair. She was dark like you. Sometimes I see her and I'm not sure if it is you. There was so little time she was with me. I see her playing beside our father's lime kiln, collecting the pretty blue flowers that grew there, her face clear and her eyes bright with life. She died when she was seven, poisoned by the bush. I was with my third husband, James Cooper, but he wasn't her father.

Middle Island 1835, James Manning

He watched Dorothea bend over the fire. She and the other one were baking seal flippers. She didn't act like a whore but that was what she was. She didn't weep either, not even when Isaac had tried to give her one. Manning had wanted to as well, but then he saw what Anderson had done to Isaac. The bastard was bowed as he stumbled back into the clearing. Anderson had walloped him in the stomach with a sealing club. It wasn't often he'd seen them fight. It was only ever over stinking women.

They were playing cards and Manning didn't like what he held in his hand. Anderson's eyes weren't on his cards either. His black forehead shone. It wasn't right that he could have three women. He was just a black bastard. He looked over at Isaac and he knew he was thinking the same. He thought back to Kangaroo Island. How Anderson's men had rowed quietly away on a still, black night, taking the well-made whaleboat with them. Isaac and Mead were left behind. Anderson had rewarded them for staying. But Manning knew why the other men didn't take Isaac. He had fought one of them and bitten off his ear.

Anderson hadn't noticed Isaac glaring at him for he was watching his woman leave the hut. Manning thought he should be allowed to have a turn with her. She'd learn something then. He smiled faintly at the thought of her lying at his feet, skirts hooked up around her thighs. But then he was disgusted. He didn't want another man's woman. She was worse, too, since Anderson had had her. She thought she could tell them all what to do. His thoughts were interrupted with Anderson leaving the table. Mead still hadn't decided what to do with the cards in his hand.

'Come on, I've had enough,' muttered Manning as he flicked his hand out onto the table.

He was so sick of it all. He looked down at the weeping red skin on his palms. And every now and then he felt the mass of white water towering over his shoulder and his muscles twitched painfully from when he had had to pull hard to keep the boat from sliding. He remembered the seals' blood which swirled thickly around his ankles, and the wind that whipped his face and his body locked cold.

He could hardly think. He was so tired he could have slept with his head in a bucket of water. When they had returned from sealing earlier in the day they had discovered that the sealer Andrews had stolen a bundle of their best skins. Manning was angry too because it meant that Anderson would be even less likely to pay him. Then Anderson had made him and Jem scrape the skins. They were forced to work alongside the black bitches, salting them and boiling up the fat on the fire. Thick clouds churned overhead and the moist granite smelt earthy. When they had finished, he held the branch back for Jem as they made their way to the well. They tried to scrape the slime and blood from their arms. He wondered then if he would ever be free of the smell of seal.

Sometimes when he and Jem lay on their bedding they talked about what they would do when they left the island. Jem said that he wanted his own boat. Then when he had enough money he would build a house on the harbour at the Sound, a house with big glass windows from where he would watch the boats coming around the point. He would smoke a pipe and drink good rum, not like that black syrupy stuff they had on the island. Manning decided that he didn't want to see or hear the sea again. He wanted dirt, good black dirt that shoots of new green could spring from. That would grow strong and produce and wither and die without being burnt and bullied by the sun and the salty wind. That was what he wanted but all he said to Jem was: 'I ain't going to be told anything by anyone.'

He watched the door of Anderson's room close behind them and he remembered the woman he once had. Except that she wasn't really a woman, just some scrawny jillet on

Kangaroo Island. When he got to the Sound he would find a white woman that didn't go with black bastards.

After Jem left the room, Manning walked out into the cold air which seemed to gust down the granite and through the trees. Anderson had known a blow was coming. The seal colony they had gone to the day before was the easiest to reach for there was a beach to haul up on. Then on the way back the wind had dropped. Their load was heavy and they struggled with the oars. Last night they had sheltered in the lee of an island but during the night the wind had turned into the northwest. They rowed towards the mainland and at dawn they followed the line of the coast, turning south when they sighted Middle Island. Then they brought in the oars and ran with the wind. But they headed a rising swell. The cloths weren't high enough and they took in water. They bailed and just when they thought they weren't going to make it, they reached the lee of Goose Island and from there the swell sank into a steady roll.

He unrolled his bedding under the verandah. It smelt of seal guts but it was better than trying to sleep in the bilge of the whaleboat, half sitting and taking turns at watches. A wind gust shook the bark cladding above him. It lifted a cup that had been left outside and it clanged against the stone. He huddled deeper into his fur. But often after sealing, instead of descending into darkness he would see the pink seal lift its head and its eye, black and glistening, would follow his steps to the boat. An hour or so later he was still unable to sleep.

He was on edge and he didn't know why. Through his mind ran confusing scenes of women and seals. They were one and then the other and sometimes they slid together skinless and unclothed, mixing and twisting so they became one. It was damp beneath his skins. In his dream Jem tossed him a thick coil of twine like the rope they would throw from the boat to the island. It would be something to hold on to.

January 1886

My life is like tumbleweed blown about in the wind. James Cooper, my third husband, was a good man. He had land next to our father at Big Grove. He was a limeburner too. But he wasn't a drinker. He kept his money and built this house on Stirling Terrace just above the harbour shore where they used to fly the Union Jack. It is two-storey and made of brick. I had a shop in the front room, downstairs. When my daughter died, it was James who took her to the surgeon's house. Although the poison was inside her, it came out in her skin. I never saw her small, sore body again.

Middle Island 1835, Dorothea Newell

She walked behind Mary and watched the way her skirt dragged in the dirt. Sea water dripped through the fabric onto the sand. Outside the hut Mary emptied the folds of her skirt of shellfish and left for the well. Dorothea entered, bare feet padding quietly across the hard surface. She took the pot off the table and hung it above the fire. When she turned around Manning was at the storeroom door. Their eyes met and he looked away.

'What are you doing?' she asked.

He hesitated by the door.

Then he walked across to the other doorway and, looking back, said: 'Left me clothes bag there.'

She stared after him, unnerved by the hate in his eyes. Hating her. She was still standing there when Mary came back.

'What's wrong?' she asked.

'I don't know,' replied Dorothea, shaking her head.

She turned to the table and cleared more plates away. They rinsed the limpets, getting rid of the furry seaweed that clung to edge of the yellow flesh, and placed the cone-shaped shells in the coals.

Later, when she went into the storeroom, she knew he had been there. And then she realised Jack's box had been moved. He had brought it to her that morning after he had loaded all his skins into the whaleboat, saying that she was to keep it. He was taking the skins to another hideout since other sealers had found this camp. Isaac and the three black women were to go with him. She thought he should take Mead instead but he said he didn't trust leaving Isaac at the camp. She had agreed then for she didn't want to be on her own with Isaac either. Anderson left midmorning without telling any of them where he was going or how long he would be. The box felt lighter but she couldn't be sure. She dared not open it. But she would speak to Manning.

That evening Anderson still wasn't back and the others were around the table. The empty shells lay in front of them like the discarded hats of miniature clowns. Dorothea didn't like it when Anderson went away but she trusted Mead. Anderson had given him one of his guns in case the sealers came back. She watched Manning. He knew because he avoided looking up. She had told Mary that she thought someone had gone through Anderson's things. She looked around the table. Jem used his knife to prise out the flesh from the last of the limpets. Yellow light from the lamp cast a shadow on one side of his face. He had changed in looks. His face seemed squarer and he grew thin tufts of reddish-brown hair from his face. He was looking more like their father and it wouldn't be long before his cheeks took on that purple hue.

She didn't want to confront Manning. There was something about him that made her uneasy. He was like a snake, thin and unpredictable. So instead she turned to them all.

'One of you has been at Jack's box. When he finds out, there'll be trouble.'

Mead tilted his head and raised his thick eyebrows. Church too looked puzzled. Manning and Jem exchanged glances.

'What are you on about?' asked Jem.

'I said someone has been at his box. If there is anything missing ...'

There was silence except for the crackling of the wood. And then Mead turned to the two lads.

'Jack'll kill the bastard.'

Manning swallowed and then grinned at Jem.

'Don't know nothing, do we?'

Jem didn't return the grin but he shook his head.

Dorothea was standing on the sandhill when Anderson returned, skirts billowing out in front of her like the sail on the whaleboat. She liked watching him. He steered the boat through the swell and caught a wave so they surfed onto the sand. Isaac leapt out over the bow and held the boat steady before it could be sucked back with the backwash. He saw her and shouted for her to get the others.

Two grey kangaroos lay damp and bloody inside the boat. Their limbs were tied to an oar and they were lifted out and taken up to the camp. Both were a good size. From the other side of the boat her eyes met Dinah's briefly. She moved closer to see what the others were looking at in the boat. It was a small wild dog, snarling and spitting. Dinah grinned.

'He like taraba. Bite.'

She showed the mark on her hand and then reached in and grabbed it by the scruff of the neck. It bared its teeth and the women chuckled gaily.

Anderson left the storeroom with the open box in his hands. His face made her feel as though her stomach had already received its blow. She clutched the top of the chair, thinking he was going to hit her with the box, but instead he threw it on the table. He leant close to her and she smelt old meat on his breath. She turned to face Mary who was on the other side of her. Their eyes met and Dorothea could see she was rigid with fear.

'My money is gone.'

The wall shimmered in front of her and in it was her brother's face. She knew that Manning had taken the money, Manning and her brother. But she couldn't say it. Then he slapped her with the back of his hand and shouted something she couldn't hear because her ear was ringing. He hit Mary on the side of the head so that she fell against her shoulder.

'Manning took your money,' Dorothea said in a flat voice, not looking at Mary, not looking at anyone.

Mead and Isaac stayed at their end of the table. Anderson drew his gun and fired it into the ceiling. Church scrambled underneath the table.

Anderson was yelling, 'I'll blow his brains out.'

Afterwards Dorothea thought he would have too if Manning had been there. They must have heard his shouting for they stayed away. But Anderson waited until they thought they were safe. When they returned that morning he pointed his gun at both of them. At first Manning claimed to know nothing. She knew this because Mary heard from Matthew what had happened. Isaac was there too. When Anderson gestured for Manning and Jem to stand before him, he asked Isaac: 'Shall I shoot them?' Isaac had grinned. Manning muttered that he could have his money and Jem's head shook. Anderson made the boys turn around and walk to the edge of the clearing. They thought he would shoot them in the back. But he didn't.

Now they were gone. And Mary blamed her. How could she do that to their brother? She watched from the sandhill as they set off in the whaleboat. The sea was sullen and flat: their bodies stick-like against it. Maybe he would shoot them later. But even though he frightened her, she sensed Anderson wouldn't do that. Matthew said she should be happy that Anderson had got his money back. But perhaps, he said, it was Manning's all along. Anderson had offered to give him fifteen pounds for working the boat but Manning said he wanted all of it. So apparently he didn't get any.

Anderson would take them to the mainland where they would be left to walk to the Sound. Dorothea didn't know how far it was but she remembered how long it took to sail. It could be the last time she saw him. She was suddenly reminded of how she had felt leaving their grandmother in Surrey. Jem was standing behind Manning. She offered her brother the seal-skin coat she had made but he turned away.

Matthew placed his arm across Mary's shoulders as they stood by the shoreline. Thin misty rain moistened their faces. The whaleboat glided further away from Goose Island. There was no wind and the oars like the legs of a spindly insect crawled across the glassy surface until it was a small dark speck in the distance. And then they were gone. Dorothea remained where she was as Mary and Matthew turned back to the camp. They passed below her. Mary glanced up, eyes dark and hard. After they had gone Dorothea stood looking out over the beach and the sea, confused. There was nothing else she could have done. She was disturbed by the way her sister had looked at her. It was as though they were strangers and she couldn't understand how it could have happened.

Low cloud covered the purple hills of Mount Arid and brought the horizon closer. So close it only just stretched to the other side of Goose Island. Everything else was hidden behind a misty curtain. The white sand was her floor, the grey sky her ceiling, the striped granite her bed, and the leathery brown seaweed washed up by the storms was her garden. And the sea rippled and pulsed like the living thing that it was, constant and unchanging. Tendrils of hair clung to her cheeks and she looked down at the moisture dripping off the ends. She wiped her face with her hands and realised they were stiff with cold.

She pushed open the door of the hut. They stopped talking and looked up. She kept her head high and warmed herself by the fire. Matthew continued.

'He said they were taking them to the bay on this side.'

'How far do you think it is to the Sound?' asked Mary.

'About four hundred miles,' replied Church.

Mary shook her head and glanced at Dorothea.

Dorothea shrugged.

'It's what they wanted.'

'It ain't. Not Jem, he didn't want to go,' said Mary, her eyes glistening. 'They took nothing with them. They won't survive.'

She blinked tears onto her cheeks. Matthew rubbed her arm. Dorothea hated him for what had so recently been forgotten. She knew Matthew held her responsible for coming between him and his wife. But how quickly he could pretend it had nothing to do with him. Instead he had been angry with Dorothea for questioning him and for sheltering Mary when she should have stayed by his side. She glimpsed in those close-set eyes his satisfaction at the way things had turned out. She turned her back then to face the fire, feeling the heat sear her eyes, causing them to water. They'd be wet and cold on the ocean, spray flicking up from the bow. Faces sticky with salt and watching. But every time she tried to see her brother's face, she saw Anderson standing above them. She tried to imagine them reaching the shore, hauling up on some sheltered bay, making tracks across the bush, arriving at the Sound, her father greeting them, glad to have his eldest son home, but still all she could see was Anderson. His proud angled face turned slightly away.

January 1886

I was alone a long time before George found me. After James died I became the strange old woman that sits in a chair by the window, watching the seasons reflected in the water. The road between my house and the harbour became busier. Mail steamers called every week and there were many more people. You wouldn't know our little King George Sound. They call it Albany town now. One day George came to my door, bringing wood to sell. He offered to collect my rent from the houses and the shop at the back. My legs were stiff. And I couldn't cross the harbour any more to Big Grove where James's other property was. George is a big man and he hates the natives but he is often in trouble for selling them grog.

Mainland 1835, James Manning

They rowed into a cove on the eastern side of Mount Arid with the silvery skin of dolphins flickering and leaping through the wake of the bow. The smiling creatures slipped from sight when the boat reached green water. The keel scraped the sand and they stepped out into brown ribbon weed that stuck to their ankles. From the beach heath-like vegetation spread dark and spiky up to the purple rocks that shone with recent rain. Cloud swirled around their peaks.

Isaac threw them a flask that splashed in the sea beside them. Jem picked it up. Anderson and his men worked the oars so they turned to face the shore.

'Hey!' Manning shouted.

Anderson looked over his shoulder.

'We need powder for a fire.'

Anderson leant down towards Isaac who brought his oar out of the water. He couldn't hear what they were saying. Then Mead nodded towards him. He waded out into the water until it was up to his chest and grasped the side of the boat, standing on his toes. Isaac handed him powder wrapped in oilskin. By the time he reached the shore and back to Jem, the whaleboat had gone around the flat rocky point.

Drizzle thickened to dense rain. Jem's brown curls were stuck to his face and water dripped from the end of his nose. Manning looked along the edge of the beach for an opening into the scrub.

'This way,' he said.

They pushed through the bush that although low was thick and hard to penetrate. Their feet sunk into wet sand. Sticks prodded their arms and legs and scratched their faces. They crawled on their hands and knees along a cut away and into a thicket of palms where the fronds splayed bright and green over their heads. They sheltered, leaning up against the thick nobbly trunks where a carpet of moss grew, and listened to the drops as they hit the leaves. Jem hadn't said anything since they left the beach. His arms were folded across the tops of his legs and he stared into the dim light.

'You alright?'

He didn't answer. Manning clenched his jaw as the cold started. It began in his fingers and then his shoulders, his feet and his thighs. He rubbed his hands on his legs and stamped his feet.

'We should keep moving.'

Jem slowly lifted his head. The look in his eyes scared Manning.

'Come on. There'll be a cave or something over the top.'

Manning crawled out of the thicket to the other side where the bush was lower and easier to walk through. He followed a kangaroo pad that twisted up over the ridge and along the line of the coast. Jem was about twenty feet behind him.

The rain kept up a steady momentum, washing their faces and watering their eyes. The big rounded rocks that could be seen from the island towered ahead. The bush clinging to the sides was tough and gnarly but occasionally there was a glimpse of colour and softness. It was low scrub, only just knee-high. Long thin roots lay above the ground to catch their feet. They climbed to a gap in the hills. From there they could see the coast as it curved around to the northwest. Across the steel-grey sea to the south was their island, the whaleboat a dark speck between them. They paused for a moment without speaking. Manning looked down at his feet. His trousers stuck to his upper legs and his lower legs were dripping with water. They would get him there. And it was better than being in a boat. It had to be.

The rain lifted. But mist edged their vision. The sand became whiter and they walked through gullies that were topped with straggly limbs and silver grass. They skirted around a lump of granite which looked from a distance as though its gullies filled with sand were folds in a pink and grey cushion. Clouds became higher and formed fat faces against a darker sky. A shaft of light shone down and moved glittering across the metallic sea. The gap in the clouds widened and bolts of yellow and mauve streaked the horizon behind the headland. The end of the bay was in shadow. A lumpy island lay close to the coast. The steep headland was covered with bush, and where it veered down towards the waterline rows of rocks like oversize tombstones stood at strange angles. And the sea slipped quietly over the flat black rocks.

They dug out burrows into the thick bush at the base of the hill. Although they shivered with cold, they didn't light a fire because they only had a small amount of powder and Manning wanted to conserve it. They had eaten shellfish that morning so they didn't need to eat and there was plenty of water. Wet black sticks crossed overhead and drops expanded and fell. They lay on black dirt that smelt of rotting vegetation. Jem jerked and muttered to himself. Manning would rather him be angry or something. It was impossible to sleep. Images of the past two years played through his mind like cards being shuffled in a pack.

The sky lightened behind black slimy branches. Manning rolled onto his stomach and the damp dirt stuck to his shirt. He edged out of the burrow and stretched. Jem was behind him. Both blackened by peaty soil. A thick blanket of clouds stretched from one horizon to the other, another shade of grey to the sand and the sea. The hills of Arid lay like a man on his back, his head pointing inland, with a round belly and legs trailing out into the ocean. Manning realised then that it was up to him. It was different from before when there had been others. He wondered what Jem was thinking.

'I'm hungry.'

Manning pointed to the rocks.

'There'll be limpets.'

'Light a fire?'

Manning shook his head.

'We should keep going,' he said. 'While we can.'

Watching Jem's face, Manning suddenly felt years older, although he probably wasn't. Not by much anyway. Jem's life before would have been different from his even though they had both been forced into work when they were young. Manning's first job had been on a merchant vessel to New Zealand as the captain's boy. By fourteen he was hanging around wharf-side taverns, thin and wiry, ready for anything. But he hadn't been ready for the crew of the *Defiance*. Before he had joined them they had dumped the body of a black woman they called their wife on an island in the Bass Strait. They hadn't found another.

Jem levered three limpets from the rock. He wrapped them in cloth and secured them around his waist. Manning also took two. But he was keen to get moving. The bush behind them was impenetrable so they retraced their footsteps from the day before. They had been covered by the tide and were now only slight indents filled with water. When the bush cleared they went inland but only to cut across the headland to the other side. They reached a wide white beach of hard sand. It was easy walking and they kept a good pace. Water ran from a creek to the sea. Although stained brown it was fresh and they filled their water flask. They dug with their knives and their hands to the root of the thick reed beside it for they knew it was good eating. They ate it raw and it filled them.

Jem seemed almost cheerful, whistling as he strode out beside Manning. The clouds were higher and there was no wind. Their pace kept them warm. The green glass water reared and rolled beside them, spreading a silky sheen on the sand as the foam slipped away from their footsteps. Black birds with red stick-like legs darted in and out and poked the wet sand with long red beaks. Black and white birds too. And there were flocks of little birds that when startled rose over the waves like a swarm of bees in perfect formation. Breakers formed several lines of foam, like layered cream on a cake, which rushed towards them over and over again.

But Manning saw only a few feet in front of him for he was thinking about what he was going to do when he reached the Sound. He had a picture in his mind of whitewashed cottages nestled comfortably in a valley between two hills overlooking a harbour that sparkled in the morning light. He would wait there for Anderson to bring in his skins and then he would get the money that was owed to him. Jem shrugged and kept walking. Manning decided that Jem didn't care.

'Don't matter that's all,' said Jem defensively. 'It's over. I don't want to have that black jack looking at me like he's going to open me up.'

Manning made a noise in his throat that sounded like a snort.

'He ain't nothing to worry about. We're here, aren't we? That was our plan.'

'It was your bleedin' plan. And we're not there. We don't even know where we're going.'

'What are you on about? Look at this.'

Manning swept his arm out wide and gestured towards the end of the beach.

'We'll be there in a few days.'

He could just make out the shape of another headland in the distance. And when he stared hard enough, he left the beach and stood in the middle of the hut on the island. His hand was resting on the table and he remembered thinking about what he was going to do. There had been a shaft of light that fell through a crack in the ceiling in front of the storeroom door. He passed through it. Inside the storeroom it was different. Since the women had been there. Shells were twisted on a line of twine across the back wall. Skins hung from the other two walls and a chest and two barrels were stacked in a corner. On the top of one of the barrels was a small chest and it had the letter R carved on its lid. He picked it up. It was a well-made oak chest with black hinges. It was heavy and when he shook it, it rattled.

He noticed the pain in his legs. It was like the muscles were pulled short. He stopped. Jem too and they looked around. He had no idea how long they had been walking but suddenly he saw that nothing had changed. Sky and more sky and a flat land and a flat sea that were like the undefined walls of a prison. Instead of a black hole, it was a bleak nothingness. They were free to move in whichever direction they fancied but they would never get anywhere and there was no other person that lived. A gull soared high overhead, catching the southerly wind draughts. Through the bird's eye he saw two ants, their nest poisoned, crawling over the endless expanse of white. Waves wiping away their prints.

That was not how it would be. No! He concentrated on the air leaving his lungs in an effort to get his breathing under control. They would not die here. He had always been conscious of the tenuous grip he had on life but never had he felt panic at the thought he might die before he reached where he was going.

Jem had stopped whistling and was watching him curiously. 'Do you think God can see us?' he asked.

Manning faced the sea. Calm again. 'Mmm.'

'Why?'

'Don't know. That's what they say,' he said as he turned back to the beach and started walking again. Jem slipped in behind him and stepped into his footsteps. After a while he called over the roar of the surf.

'Don't you think that even for Him we're too far away?'

Manning shrugged. He didn't know what he thought. He stepped on the little brown balls like peas that popped. Then he slowed and walked beside him.

'Tell me what it was like in England.'

'Don't remember much,' said Jem and then he lifted his head. 'We had a house on the edge of the green. It was a big house and my grandmother lived in the front. It was her house when my granddad was alive. We moved there after Mother had William. He was the seventh.'

Jem paused.

'Then the overseer told me dad that he couldn't afford to pay him.'

'For what?'

'For harvesting the corn.'

'You had no money?'

'Me dad sold the grandmother's house.'

Manning was picturing Jem's family. Seven children. He only knew that his mother came out on the convict ship *Hero*. He didn't know where she was from or what she had done, just that her belly was big with a child when she reached Botany Bay. She had died a few years later with the effort of trying to produce another fatherless infant. Manning was made a ward of the new state and looked after by the Benevolent Asylum. He had a friend, a small girl. They would go down to the creek and play amongst the rocks, skimming pebbles across the clear surface. On hot humid days they would discard their rags and splash and paddle in the shallows. It was their secret until the matron found them. She reminded him of a crow. Always in black and with a large pendant at her neck. Her eyes flickered darkly and she had the same ability to make him feel that there was evil about. On that particular day his friend was whipped and sent out into the street. He knew she was only a child and until now he had never thought of her.

When he had been paid his share of the ship's lay, he would wander between the dockside inns. He would drift between crews he had worked with and other boys who lived the better part of their lives on the sea. That was when he had learnt about women.

⁓

The sun was low in the sky and it was a sickly glow behind grey clouds that threatened rain. Thankfully the rain had held off. They reached the end of the beach and the mouth of a wide river that was salty. The soles of his feet felt flattened and burnt at the edges. They ate the remaining flag-reed root and drank their water. Green-eyed flies settled on their ankles and pierced their flesh with long thin spikes.

⁓

After days of being battered by bush and climbing rocks, they were exhausted and low in spirits. And on top of that it was beginning to rain again. In the distance they could see steep rocky hills which reared up in awkward shapes and angles from the grey-green matted scrub that covered the contour of the land. As they neared them, the colours of the rock changed from a nondescript purple to stripes of black and brown and orange and slithers of silver marked where water had run from the recent rain. Caves near the summit were like yawning mouths which provided a lofty retreat for the birds.

Manning had a sore in the arch of his foot which was making him irritable. Jem said he thought they had reached the place where the *Mountaineer* had run aground. Manning said they would have passed it days ago. But Jem insisted and then when he predicted a freshwater lake just behind the next sandhill Manning had to accept he was right. They also argued whether they should go inland to cut across the headland. Manning wanted to know how he knew it would be a shortcut. Jem claimed to remember the deep indented bay from before. Manning grudgingly gave in but with the condition that they took from the rocks as many limpets as they could carry in case they got lost.

The bush cleared and they climbed over gently undulating granite that had collected the latest shower in little pools of sweet water. But the constant exposure to moisture in the air and the puddles on the ground made their skin wrinkled like old men. Manning thought that if he were squeezed he would ooze liquid like a cloth wrung dry. The rock dipped and water rushed over it and down through reeds and bush on the other side. They collected more of the root of the rust-coloured reed and wrapped it in cloth. To their left rose a ridge of granite that was perhaps forty to fifty feet high. There were crevices and caves but they would be difficult to get to. But then through the bush they glimpsed the dark hole of a ground-level cave. Manning pushed aside the red flowered shrub and crawled underneath a spiky tree and into the dry dark interior.

Once inside they were still for a moment. Their minds and bodies numb with exhaustion, listening to the drops of rain splatter on the leaves outside. The rock where they had just come from was covered in mist, and water drops from the mouth of the cave increased to streams. Manning started to shake with cold. Jem clenched his jaw tight to stop his teeth from chattering. They moved to the back of the cave, finding dry leaves and branches blown in by a storm. They heaped them into a pile with a small amount of their precious powder. After several attempts Manning produced a spark from friction between two rocks and ignited the powder that lay amongst the leaves. They started to crackle and smoulder. Jem crawled out and collected more wood. Eventually their fire brightened and began to produce heat. They had almost forgotten what it felt like. It lit the walls of the cave, which were smooth and striped. It wasn't high enough to stand but it went quite a way back so they could escape from the smoke but still enjoy the warmth. They cooked the limpets in their shells and roasted the roots. They had never tasted so good.

They built up the fire so that it wouldn't go out and lay down in the soft dry sand. Manning had a vague sense that his body ached but his mind was in another place. Jem's coughing woke him. It was dark outside and the fire had burnt down to a few glowing coals. He put more wood on and gently blew the flame into life. When he touched Jem to give him some water he discovered his skin was burning.

He wasn't any better the next day. His face was flushed and his eyes were glassy. He moaned a lot and wheezed a deep harsh cough and then slept. Manning supported his neck while he sipped water from the flask. He soaked a piece of cloth and wiped his forehead. But most of the time he sat listening to the sound of his rasping breath. Outside the sky was clear of cloud and the air, fresh and crisp. He didn't want to leave him but he couldn't sit there any longer either. So he went down to the sea for limpets. It would be the route they would take when Jem was well. He dared not think that he might be doing it on his own.

The bush was about head height and thick in places. He cut some of it with his knife so that it would be easier next time. He reached the beach when the sun was at its highest and noticed a thin column of smoke a little way inland. It would be natives. Even though they might be hostile, the sign of human life was a comfort. Then he looked along the beach and it seemed to go on forever. It was more of the same. They weren't any closer to anywhere. Perhaps it would all be like that. He wouldn't even know the Sound when he reached it. And then he thought bleakly that the Swan River could be the same. He shook his head. What was wrong with him? How could it be anything but paradise? There he would have the chance to be someone else. But he needed money.

Through the salt spray were islands. He sat quite still on the sloping rock and stared into it, his eyes shifting focus. The haze became like a curtain and it cleared and he saw light through the flickering leaves of trees. A cool peppermint-scented place and moist grass that glistened on the banks of a slow-moving river. A woman spread her arms out wide and she was beautiful with long black hair and red lips. And she settled on the water and folded her arms beside her and her long neck moved with a body that glided with the tide.

On a nearby rock a big black and white gull lowered its head and its neck began to wobble as it collected the air to sound its laughter. He looked up into its cold hard stare. The gull's call brought its mate and they stood a little way off with their heads to the side as though they were as dis-interested as he was. But he knew their mean little eyes were on his limpets. He picked up a rock and threw it at one of them. Its wings lifted it a little way off the ground and it settled again, as unconcerned as before. He didn't even matter to a seagull.

When he returned to the cave Jem had improved. He sat at the fire that had been stoked into a healthy blaze. Together they ate the succulent yellow flesh of the limpets. When it was cooked in the shell, the meat was tender. Raw it was tough like boot leather and it left a strange taste in the mouth. But it was better than nothing. His friend's cheeks had lost their fullness and the hair on his face was thin and patchy. There were sores in the corners of his mouth. But his eyes were clear and they looked directly back into Manning's.

'What's it like?' he asked. 'Where we're headed.'

Manning shrugged and lifted the shell of the limpet up to his mouth, draining the watery contents.

'Half a mile to the beach. Then the beach curves around. Can't see for how long.'

Jem coughed and it rattled in his chest.

Manning looked up.

'You alright?'

Jem nodded.

'Leave tomorrow?'

He nodded again.

Cicadas clicked outside. Flies whined by the entrance. A fresh breeze from the south blew the smoke into their faces. Manning moved and leant against the wall on the side; from there he could see out across the bush to the sea and the purple islands that wavered in the distance. Jem's voice roused him from his doze.

'You know, I ain't ever been with a woman.'

Manning opened one eye.

'I don't want to die not knowing what it's like.'

'Who says you're going to die?'

Jem traced lines in the sand with a stick. Manning watched the lines like snake trails move around the floor of the cave and thought that perhaps they would be the only sign that they had ever been here. And then he wondered who would find them.

It became harder to rid his mind of black thoughts. After they left the heart-shaped bay, the beaches were shorter and interrupted with steep rocks to climb and stunted and deformed scrub to push through. They had to go inland often but never too far that they lost sight of the sea, and they were torn and scratched by inhospitable sticks and branches and roots. What they needed were small axes but they had only their knives. Often they passed a mob of kangaroos and they would be tormented with the memory of succulent roo flesh. But they couldn't think of a way to kill them. A couple of times they tried catching seagulls with snares made from the cloth of their trousers, but it was hopeless. They had used all their powder so they had no means to make a fire.

He began to dream of the black-haired woman. She would turn slowly and beckon with one hand, the feathery ends of her hair reaching her knees and covering her breasts. Her body was white, and blue veins cast a map beneath her skin. But when he looked to her face her lips blurred and became like blood, like raw meat. The pain in the centre of his belly made him feel as though his guts would spill out. When he woke there was only flag-reed root or limpets to eat.

As they trod gingerly through the scrub Jem would describe the feast he had dreamt about until Manning would have to tell him to stop. And then he would chew on the wallaby skin he wore around his shoulders. But he lacked the strength in his jaws to penetrate the stiff salty hide.

They became weaker, resting at greater intervals, but the cold seemed to find its way in so that they were never warm. They shivered when they stopped and became exhausted by their shivering. It was then that Jem became like a child, constantly whining about their journey and pleading with Manning to tell him when it would end.

When they rested beneath a bush, Manning decided that he wanted to stay. That there would be nothing easier than to lie down beneath its gnarled branches that smelt sharply of citrus and to never get up again. The pain left his body and he was at peace. But Jem's voice, like the blunt edge of a knife on a piece of hide, gradually worked its way through his consciousness and forced him to rally his spirits. Then it struck him that he would not die sooner by having hope. And he had to be hopeful for Jem.

January 1886

When it is night I touch the skin under his arms. It is soft and smooth, like silk. Not like the skin on his shoulders which was hardened by the sun. I can see his face when he is refusing to smile. He is good at revealing nothing. Like a stone. He walks sometimes that slow measured walk around my house. He never saw our daughter. He was murdered the year she was born. A sealer told me that they had found Jack's body on Mondrain Island. He had been shot through the head and they killed Dinah too. I know that island for it is a day's sailing from Middle Island. We would shelter there on our way to the Sound.

Jack believed in the other world, that there were restless souls who wandered. Sometimes I wonder if he were not dead before I knew him. When the natives first saw white people, they believed we were their ghosts. I wonder what they thought of Jack.

Middle Island 1835, Dorothea Newell

When Anderson returned he didn't say anything about Jem. It was dark when they hauled up on the beach and the three men came through the trees without speaking. Matthew and Mary had left for their tent. Earlier, when she had gone outside for water, she had noticed that a fire burnt brightly in front of it. Church had remained in the hut and for that she was grateful. Dinah had been in before and brought with her a tammar she had snared. Dorothea had skinned it and it was roasting over the fire. When the meat began to brown she wondered about Jem and what he would be eating.

Dorothea looked up and he didn't look at her. Instead he came in and continued through and into the other room. Isaac sat behind her and Mead pulled a chair close to the fire. Eventually she turned to Mead who looked up and smiled a half-smile.

'Smells good.'

'Where are they?'

The warmth left his eyes.

'On the mainland, at the base of them hills.'

'Will they … will they be alright?' she asked without turning away from the fire.

Mead shrugged: 'They got plenty of water and as long as they stay on the coast they got shellfish.'

Then Anderson was behind her and he looked over her shoulder and down at the cooked meat.

'Serve it up, woman.'

She listened to their talk around the table. There had been a sea elephant on one of the flat rock islands close to the coast. Which, reckoned Mead, was unusual for around here. He had been on an English whaler in the Bass Strait and they had brought in a southern right to cut up and try out on the beach. Camped on the island were a group of sealers. There was a fellow, he said, that had a sea elephant as a pet.

'It's the truth. It was about thirty feet long and about eighteen feet wide. This fellow he'd be stroking it and feeding it. He'd hop on its back or it'd follow him around like a dog. Its big ugly snout waving about. When he was full of grog he got in a fight and some bastard killed him. The sea elephant that is, not him,' said Mead with a grin.

Anderson didn't seem to be listening and neither was Isaac. Church was the only one who appeared interested. Isaac had a mean look and it wasn't just towards her. He seemed to be directing it at everyone, or perhaps it was mostly towards Anderson. She hoped he was on his guard. But then she watched Anderson staring across the table to the wall on the other side, his eyes unfocused, and she wondered why she cared. What he had done to her brother was unforgivable. He was a brute, a savage brute.

Abruptly Anderson stood up and muttered something to himself but they all heard it.

'The man hath penance done, and penance more will do.'

Church raised his eyebrows and stared at the empty doorway through which Anderson had just gone.

'Coleridge?' he asked with an odd look on his face.

And then after a while he shook his head slowly. Dorothea realised something had happened but she wasn't sure what. The others were quiet too. Church's mouth was forming words without sound.

⁓

When she trod the path to the well she sensed his presence through the warmth of his body and then she saw his outline against the bush. A man created in the image of Adam. She didn't know why she thought that but it suddenly came to her. His arms enveloped her and he drew her close to his chest, her head resting against his skin and the skin of an animal. She could hear the beat of his heart. Steady. They stood like that for a moment, her body tense until gradually it lost its resistance and she yielded to him, and it reminded her of the times when she sat in the sun and the heat made her dopey and senseless. Then he let her go and left her in the dark.

She heard movement outside the door of the storeroom and then there was silence and the sound of the sea, as familiar now as her own breathing. Then she heard another sound, the lonesome howl from the pup captured and brought across the sea by Dinah. But there were no dogs to hear its cry.

⌒

She knelt in the clearing beside Dinah. The sky was pale blue and a cold breeze blew down the rock from the south and stiffened their fingers. Dinah and Sal had brought back five tammars that they had snared on the fork of a well-worn pad. Their snares were made out of strong yarn from canvas threads rubbed together. They were about eighteen inches long with a slipknot tied at one end. The snare was like a noose that was stretched out on two small y-shaped sticks and put across the tammar pads or trails to catch the animals around the neck. As the slipknot tightened they would choke to death.

Dinah explained how they worked with her hands. Then she said the skins make very good shoes, very good to wear. She asked Dorothea if she wanted some. Dorothea nodded. Dinah dislocated the limbs of the tammar and explained that it was so the spirits couldn't run away. She cut off the tails at the stump. Then she skinned the largest one with almost a flick of her wrist. She gestured to Dorothea to place her feet over the fresh warm skin. Dinah moulded it to her foot and cut it and stitched the two ends at the top with the animal's tendon. She did the same with the other foot. And then removed them for drying.

The small yellow dog sniffed around their feet for meat. And taking hold of a piece of skin with its sharp little teeth, it growled and tugged until it got what it wanted. Then it lay in the dirt, chewing and playing with its find. Dorothea reached down and rubbed its neck. It lifted its head and playfully snapped at her fingers. Dinah was watching and they both smiled.

The women skinned the rest of the animals and stretched the skins over sticks to dry. It was pretty silvery-grey fur with reddish-brown patches across the shoulders. Dorothea collected the tails of the animals and soaked them in boiling water until the fur could be scraped off easily and then placed them in the hot ashes in the hearth where they would cook slowly for several hours. She had also learnt that from Dinah. At first she had been uncomfortable with her light-footed presence. But then she got used to it and it made up in some way for Mary's continued silence. She thought that maybe Matthew was responsible for the way Mary was acting. He had his wife back and he wasn't going to let Dorothea come between them again.

Sometimes she wondered if Anderson had lain with Dinah and Sal before she came to the island. She wanted to know but most of the time she didn't have the will to find out. Rules elsewhere held no meaning for her. After a while she sought out the company of the black women and felt emboldened by the knowledge they shared with her.

So when Mooney asked for her hair she gave it willingly. The others sat in a semicircle around her while Dinah used the sharpened edge of an abalone shell to cut it. It was very long, almost to her waist and it had become a matted mess. Dinah hacked through it and cut close to her scalp, the brown coils falling in the dirt. The women reached forward, picking up pieces, holding it up to the light and then from end to end, admiring its length. Mooney collected it all in a bundle and then thinned it out with her fingers. She picked up two small twigs about four inches long and placed one across the other in the form of a cross. Then she rubbed the strands of Dorothea's hair across her bare thigh and when it was thick enough she wound it around the sticks and it became a thick reel of strong twine. That way she could store it in her skin pouch and use it when she needed it.

When Dorothea stood up, her neck felt cold and exposed. But her head was unburdened and she shook it. They watched her. Then she smiled and they all smiled. That evening Anderson ran his big broad hand over her scalp and chuckled and told her she looked like a boy. But Anderson was different since the night he had returned to her bed.

It was a few days after the boys had left. She had hardly seen him. He would leave the hut before light and return after dark but she knew he didn't leave the island. That night she woke, startled, staring up into the darkness, not seeing but knowing that his bulk was only just above her. She was frozen with fear for she thought he had come to harm her, and her breathing was tight and shallow. But instead he leant back on his heels and shushed her.

'Let me lie with you,' he said. 'I want to feel your goodness.'

He lowered himself onto his side and his body was pressed hard against her side. She could see now that he faced her, his head rested on the palm of his hand. She lay on her back, arms by her side, and gradually her breathing became more regular and she noticed his smell which was strong but not unpleasant. He brought his other hand up to her neck and lightly traced the contours of her cheek and jawline.

'You're the first white woman, I ever had.' And he chuckled. 'But it's all the same in the dark.'

He paused and when he spoke again his tone had changed.

'But it ain't, is it? Not like it says in the Bible. That we are all children of the same parent,' he added bitterly. 'That's a story for children.'

She listened to the scratching of an animal on the other side of the wall.

'Where I come from it's against the law. A black can't love a fair woman because their children will be brown.'

Instead of sounding angry, his voice was soft and regretful. He sighed and then he started again.

'When I was a boy my father was an old man. A British sailor owned him. But he was freed after his ship was captured off New England. So he went to live in Hartford. There were other free blacks there and they elected him leader. I was named after him. He wanted us to be good Americans. Good black Americans. He always said that we would earn the respect of our white neighbours if we worked hard and were sober and honest.'

He laughed then. A harsh-sounding laugh that startled her for his voice had been like a lullaby. She hadn't really been listening to the words.

'But we couldn't go to school with their children. Nor could we sit with them at church. The old man wasn't beaten though. He had his own school and our book was the Bible.'

He paused then and breathed deeply as though the burden had grown heavier.

But he just muttered: 'He was a foolish old man.'

He brought his hand down, which had been resting in the curve of her neck, to her stomach and rubbed it as though he wanted to erase the past.

'What am I saying? What is this story I'm telling? The albatross I wear round my neck is black,' he said with a quiet fierceness.

Then he stroked her lightly across the ribs and her heart beat quickly beneath them. He lifted her skirt and when he was done he lay on her with his head buried in the soft skin of her neck. He slept with her that night and she woke to his arm across her belly and his eyes on her face.

'I will buy you a beautiful gown,' he said.

⁓

After that it was as though he had said all he had wanted to say. There was much about him that puzzled her but she didn't know the questions to ask. The weather had become distinctly wintery with stormy squalls that brewed in the south and spat slanting rain. But between the storms there were days of calm, of sparkling stillness when the sun caught the sea's brilliance and the white edges of the island. The mind cleared like the pale crystal water and smoothed away the ripples. The men and the black women would go sealing then. And she would be left on the island with Church and her sister.

It was hard now because Mary continued to build the wall between them. Her outrage became her armour and she never weakened. Dorothea was lonely. And Mary must have been too. At first she had tried to explain that Anderson wasn't bad. That he wasn't like the others. But Mary didn't want to listen. Dorothea sometimes felt that the silence screamed between them. Didn't Mary realise they were all safer if she was with

Anderson? After a while she began to see that it was more than just Anderson and her betrayal of Jem. Mary had sprung into life. She suddenly seemed to have found a purpose. It made her stronger. Her helplessness had turned to anger and she directed it towards Dorothea because she could.

So on those days Dorothea would find work in the camp: bringing rocks from the granite to line pathways, or she might rake up the leaves that lay under the trees. There was always water seeping from the rock so she would dig gullies to head it off into the sand, and then there was the garden. Sometimes, though, she would just walk along the beaches and over the rocks, collecting shells and watching the birds. Then she would sit and feel on her head the weak winter sun when it was high in the sky. And the sea's currents would run one way and then another.

It was on one of those days that she found a beach of shells. Beautiful, intricate art forms washed up from the deep. The little beach faced east and jagged black rocks lay between it and the rolling swell. They would break over a large square-shaped boulder and the white spray would shoot high above it. But where she knelt it was protected. She wondered how the shells had got there. How they could be deposited by such a violent sea and remain unbroken. They must be stronger than they looked, she thought. Her hands sifted through them and she discovered a treasure-trove of coloured coral and spotted molluscs. Coral that was pink and purple and orange. Tiny fronds punctured with holes that dried hard. Shells, browns and dusky pinks, which were striped and washed with the colour of sunset. She collected a bundle of the best of them and wrapped them in the folds of her shawl.

She retraced her steps, walking around the long narrow headland instead of continuing to an area of the island she hadn't been before. As she came over the flat rock she could see the whaleboat sailing into the other end of the beach in front of the camp. She hesitated for a moment, unsure at first as to whether it was Anderson. Reassured by his dark silhouette standing tall at the stern, she continued down onto the beach.

She reached them as they hauled up on the sand. Sal remained in the boat as they lifted it up to the sandhill, her head bent down to her chest. Anderson acknowledged her with a quick glance and got on with the business of unloading the dripping skins. But the two black women stayed at the side of the boat and reached in to help Sal. They half dragged and lifted her and although it was clear that she was in pain she made no sound. Dorothea followed a little way behind as they carried her up to their camp and laid her down.

On Sal's leg was a gaping wound that revealed the white of her bone. Against her black skin, her red flesh was startling. Dorothea sat beside Dinah who was chanting in her language and separating pieces of bark. Mooney left with her digging stick and wooden trough.

'What happened?' she asked. Her hands supported her as she knelt on the ground. She couldn't look directly at the wound and so she watched Dinah. Dinah explained that Sal's leg had been jammed between the rock and the boat by a wave. Mooney returned with a bowlful of slow-moving larvae. She crushed them with her digging stick and packed them into the wound. Dorothea turned away as her mouth filled with the acid of her guts and she coughed. She got up then but looked back over her shoulder as Dinah wrapped Sal's leg with bark.

When she walked through the door Mead was talking about his encounter with a bull seal. No one seemed to be listening but that didn't stop him. Anderson had laid out slabs of seal meat for cooking and she began to prepare it for roasting.

'Sal is hurt badly,' she said.

Anderson shrugged.

'Stupid black bitch got in the way,' said Isaac and he flicked his head in the direction of Anderson. 'He's got two of them anyway.'

Then he grinned, his yellow moist grin. She looked at Anderson. He was staring into the fire and when he noticed, he frowned.

'What's wrong with you?' he asked crossly.

She shook her head slightly but she kept her gaze on him. He picked up a cup and threw it against the stone at the back of the fireplace. It clanged and dropped into the ashes. They looked at him.

'Daft bitches,' he muttered and left the room.

When she lay with him that night, she asked whether he had taken them into his bed. He didn't speak and she thought he was angry that she had gone too far.

'It ain't the same,' he said after a while. 'They don't have feelings.'

She thought about what he said. She couldn't remember when she had begun to notice the women and the way they talked to each other. She listened to the sounds in their language which could be flat and sad and at other times sweet and high. She saw how they looked after one another. She felt how they suffered and sensed that it was eased a little by the strength of their companionship. If Sal died, she had no doubt that Dinah would too. She knew too that they carried a heavy sadness and a longing for something. She didn't know what it was. She thought perhaps it was family. She asked Dinah one day and discovered it was more than that. But Dinah found it impossible to explain in white man's language. She knew Anderson was wrong. But then she was only a woman, what did she know?

⌒

The southerly wind had strengthened the next morning. She wrapped her seal-skin coat around her and put on her shoes, thinking as the soft fur of the tammar caressed the soles of her feet that they were the most comfortable she had ever worn. She took with her the seal meat and walked through the trees to where her sister and Matthew were camped. Mary looked up as she tended her fire. It lay between them.

'I have some meat for you,' she said.

Mary's mouth tightened.

'We have some. Matthew brought it yesterday.'

Dorothea sighed and stood with the plate out in front of her.

'Does it have to be like this?'

'Like what?' shrugged Mary.

'You know what I mean.'

'Nothing's changed,' said Mary. 'Except you. Look at you. You look like a savage.'

Dorothea's fingers tightened around the dish and she fought the urge to scream. She wanted to yell that she was sick of looking out over the rock, the beach, the mainland that never got any closer. She was sick of it all too but what was there to do? She hated the island. The ugly black streaks in the rock and the mess of broken shells left by the gulls and the dead-looking spindly shrubs that edged it and were bent over by the wind like old hags.

Instead she turned away and went back to the hut where she came across Dinah and Mooney collecting wattle seeds. She asked after Sal.

'Very bad,' said Dinah, shaking her head, and her eyes were large in her face.

Sal rested on a skin beneath the paperbark dome. The fire smouldered weakly beside her. She raised her head and smiled at Dorothea and then slumped back in the dirt. Dinah squatted at the fire and poked the wattle pods into the ashes.

'She my sister,' said Dinah sadly.

Dorothea sometimes found her English hard to follow. But from what she understood, Dinah and Sal were of the same family from an island across the sea. Another man had taken them. Not Anderson, she said, a very bad man who hurt them a lot. Dorothea remembered the shells she had collected and she gave Sal the one she had liked the most. Her hot hand held it tightly and her eyes moved to Dorothea's face but she lay still.

When she returned to their camp two days later, Sal was sitting in front of the dome and had tied the shell around her neck. Her eyes were clear but she couldn't stand on her own. They offered Dorothea some hot seeds to eat, which they shelled from the wattle pods like peas, except they were black. The little dog growled and sniffed around them and chewed on a stick. Dinah picked it up and cradled it in her arms and it licked her hands. She grinned.

'He good now, very happy. Look here. He fat,' she said, rolling him over.

Dorothea nodded but she wanted to know something. If Anderson hadn't taken them from their home then how did they come to be with him? Dinah stared sideways and back. She let the dog go and rubbed the heel of her hands over her thighs which were grey with ash.

She muttered to herself for a bit and then said: 'Big fight.'

'Where?'

'Island.'

Dorothea asked her to explain and as she listened to her words, spat like the husks of the seeds, she began to piece together the story. It seemed that the man who captured them was the leader of a large sealing gang. They had a camp on a small island a long way to the east. She and Sal were forced to swim in water where there were sharks, and when they weren't hunting or cooking they were tied to the fireplace by a long chain. Then a big black man, who was Anderson, appeared one day. They didn't know where he came from but he was very hungry. Instead of giving him food, their master flogged him. His clothes were taken from him and he was tied with the women. But when they came back from sealing he was gone. The chain was broken and their master was very angry. Dinah looked sideways and rubbed her arms.

'What happened?'

'Jack, he come back in the night. He kill him.'

'Oh,' said Dorothea.

～

She watched Anderson at the fireplace. She watched the way his body reflected the firelight as he turned. He looked up under his brow and his eyes were warm. But she looked away. She noticed the rough edges of the timber and the ants that drew a line from the roof to the floor and where they went to after that she had no idea. Anderson lit the lamp on the table. Mead and Isaac were playing cards. She didn't know where Church was.

Anderson came around behind her and placed his hands on her shoulders. It was nearly a month since he had left Jem and Manning on the mainland. She wondered if they were dead.

Then it would be at least three people she knew of who would have died by Anderson's hand. Her neck stiffened and she stared straight ahead. It wouldn't take much for him to wrap his big hands around her and squeeze the life from her. In some ways she wished he would. Then he stroked the sides of her bare neck with his thumbs and she shivered. His thick dry lips were beside her ear and his voice rumbled through her.

She couldn't refuse him. Although as he led her into his room she wondered what would happen if she did. Would he harm her? Despite what she had learnt about him, somehow she couldn't imagine it. His touch was too soft.

Later she lay on her side facing him, his arm tucked around the hollow of her back. He wasn't asleep and neither was she. The wind lifted the cladding. They wouldn't be sealing tomorrow. He stroked the curve of her hip and her face rested on the hard skin of his shoulder. And when he breathed her head rose slightly. She was thinking about what Dinah had told her. If the story was true. But it would be. Then she realised that it didn't matter. His breathing changed and she knew he was asleep. His muscles twitched, sometimes quite violently, and they jerked her head. She moved away from him and he rolled onto his side, facing away from her.

⁓

She stepped over the water that ran from the rock. It had carved gullies in the dirt. The black soil was sticky and waterlogged, the granite shiny with rain. Awkwardly she held an armful of damp firewood, the sticks rubbing dirt onto the front of her gown. She shivered and her hands were covered with wrinkles that were black lines crossing her palms.

When she stood in front of the fire, her gown steamed. She took off her shoes and turned them towards the fire. Her toes were numb. Her gown stuck to her like a second skin for since being on the island she had never taken it off to wash. The grey coarse cotton was soiled and torn. She had grown used to it but suddenly it had become unbearable.

She noticed Anderson in the doorway. She remembered him washing clothes in a barrel that had the top cut off. She asked where it was. He offered to help for there was nothing to do when it rained. He brought it in and placed it in front of the fire. She decided then that she would wash as well. If she sat with her knees bent she would be able to have a bath. Anderson told her there was whale lye she could use for soap.

The first pot of water steamed over the fire.

'I need to bring it in there,' she said, pointing to his room.

Although there wasn't anyone about, she could hear voices from under the verandah.

He raised his brow.

'I want to take off my gown,' she said, knowing that with him she was safe.

He dragged the barrel into the other room and filled it with hot water. They heated some more until there was about a foot and half steaming at the bottom. He brought in the lamp and placed it on the wooden chest. After he closed the door she removed her gown and her undergarment that had once been white. He stood in the shadow, leaning against the door. Moist, warm air filled the room and his face glistened. Rain thumped on the roof and drips splatted on the ground beneath the eaves. Naked, she looked up at him and smiled slightly.

The yellow light was kind to her skin and she glowed. Her nipples were dark and erect like a seal's. She moved deliberately, and slowly filled with a strange, tingling lightness. She knew she could do anything and that she was safe. She didn't look at him again, not directly, for there was no need, for every inch of her skin soaked his gaze and it was nourishment. Like the whale lye she rubbed over her skin and into her breasts. She stood up, rubbing it between her legs.

Still he remained in the shadow. She bent over and scrubbed the gown, wringing it out and hanging it over the side. Then she knelt and scooped the water over her face and her hair, eyes closed as the warm liquid caressed her skin and ran down her neck and dripped off the end of her breasts. Lightly, he took the drip with his fingers and her nipples puckered. She looked down at his hands, which had come from behind. And with his arms under hers, he gently raised her out of the water. Her body leant against his and he was naked and hard against her. She was wet when he lay her down and their bodies fused moistly. Her skin was pink and soft. She was warm and expansive, a woman who could nurture and forgive.

⌒

While her gown dried over the fireplace, they lay in the other room wrapped in skins, feeling as though they were the only ones who existed. But then over the top of the sound of the waves they would be disturbed by the sound of Isaac's barking laugh or Mead's steady drone. The water had long gone cold in the tub when she asked him about what Dinah had said. The crows on the other side of the wall spoke tonelessly to one another. The light wavered on the ceiling. They didn't really need a lamp but it gave them a feeling of warmth and security, as though they were enclosed in a cocoon that no one could penetrate.

He sighed deeply and then began to speak: 'The story is too long. You have to know the beginning to know the end.'

He paused and looked up at the ceiling.

'I think it is better to be ignorant: to not know of God's promises. The British sailor, he taught my father to read. My father thought it was a gift. For me it has been a curse. That's not what you want to know, is it?'

He smiled and placed his hand over her arm.

'I'll start with when I went to sea. I was to be paid at least. But there was hatred too. We were packed in the forecastle and fed hard tack and salt junk. The first time it was four years.'

'If you could read, why did you go to sea?' she asked quietly and to show she was listening.

His hand left her arm to clasp his other hand across his chest.

'On a whaler green hands are paid the same for they take the same risks.'

He turned sideways and took her hand again.

'So I sailed again. This time as a boatsteerer. After twelve months we anchored in a bay at Paita. I went ashore with two others for supplies. I didn't return. There was too much sickness. Then I joined an English whaler heading for Sydney. I had a berth in the cabin. The captain had many books. I read them all. I was happy then.

'We took whales near Van Diemen's Land. One night the moon was high and bright, it was my watch, four men, one of them, the first mate, came from behind and bound my hands and legs. They threw me overboard.'

'Why?'

He was silent and his eyes closed for a moment. She turned sideways and saw the pain in his face.

'I offended them. Black men don't sit at the captain's table and talk poetry. They sing sea shanties and make people laugh.'

She watched the way his lips met when he spoke; they brushed lightly and then squashed together.

'What happened?' she asked.

'I should have drowned. I don't remember. I untied my hands. I stayed afloat. We were in the lee of an island. I drifted towards it. I was lucky I could swim.'

His eyes flickered and she knew he was reliving the experience. His hand tightened its grip on her arm and he turned to look at her. Wide- and yellow-eyed. He didn't need to tell her any more. She remembered when the *Mountaineer* had run aground at Thistle Cove. It was night and the ocean had been a thin liquid sheet that covered the depths of hell.

'It is easier to be what people expect you to be,' he said quietly, before hauling himself up. She was surprised that his buttocks were lighter than his back. Raised purple welts crossed his skin like the seams of quartz that ran through the granite. It seemed that his story had ended.

That evening they ate in front of the fire with moisture seeping in under the door. It hadn't stopped raining all day. But her gown was crisp and clean and it felt like fabric again. She felt softer and lighter. Stew simmered above the fireplace and filled the hut with savoury smells. Dorothea went to make bread and discovered they had finished the *Mountaineer*'s flour. She stood at the doorway. He had his back to her. When she spoke he turned around.

'There's no flour, Jack.'

He nodded.

'The molasses is finished too,' she said.

Isaac looked up and watched Anderson's face and then he said: 'We've enough skins to fill the boat again.'

Anderson stared thoughtfully ahead for a moment. Then he looked from one to the other and shook his head.

'Too much of a risk. Another couple of months and the winds will have changed.'

But for Dorothea that suddenly signalled hope. It meant there was to be an end to this timeless, featureless existence they had been living now for almost half a year. She stored that knowledge in her mind and it was like something precious she could put away and retrieve at anytime, which she could quietly examine and polish so that it shone.

⁓

The first thing she did the next day was to tell Mary that they would be leaving.

'How soon?' she asked coldly.

'He said in a month or two. I'm sure I can get him to leave sooner.'

Mary shrugged and pushed the oily strands of hair from her face. She turned her back and lifted the flap of the canvas, disappearing inside the tent.

Dorothea continued down onto the granite. The breeze that blew across the island from the south ruffled the sea's surface and lightly brushed the curls on top of her head. The rain had cleared but there were still fat clouds hanging low in the distance. Every now and then the sun broke through and brightened the sea's colour. She sat on the rock that sloped to the water and watched the weed in the shallows swaying with the swell. A Pacific gull settled nearby and seemed to peer at her from the corner of its red-rimmed eye.

She hadn't dared to let herself think about the future. But now he had said he would take the whaleboat to the Sound, it meant she was free to see the way back. There was, though, the memory of reaching the island. But she had more faith in Anderson than she had had in Jansen. What had become of him and the others, she wondered. The sea was as bland and as secretive as ever. There was no way of knowing who had been before. The tide might shift sand so that beaches changed shape, but the sea's surface was eternal. It enveloped the unmarked graves of men and the wrecks of their ships so that any lesson to be learnt lay hidden beneath the waves.

The Pacific gull lifted off the ground and settled a short distance away on a large boulder. It was often to be found there, its head turned to the sea, its white waste splattered on the rock beside it. She looked up and saw that it was Anderson who had disturbed it. He sat beside her.

She wondered what he intended for her. Did he expect her to return to the island with him? That was asking too much.

'What will happen, Jack?'

'What do you mean?'

'To us. Afterwards?'

He didn't say anything but his expression hardened and he looked more like the man she had met on the beach months ago. His head turned slightly and she realised he was watching someone. She followed the direction of his gaze and caught a glimpse of Isaac as he disappeared over the other side of the sandhill, further down the beach.

'What's wrong?' she asked as he stood up.

'He has my gun,' he said. 'No one takes my gun.'

The way he said it caused her stomach to contract. Anderson usually wore his pistols but since Manning and Jem had gone he had taken to leaving the brace beside the wooden chest in his room. She didn't trust Isaac and she wondered how he came to be working for Anderson. What would he do? She knew he was capable of the worst, and that was killing Anderson and taking them all as his own.

'He's probably just gone after a pigeon.'

Anderson showed no sign that he had heard and, frowning, he walked across the rock back to the camp, occasionally looking over to where Isaac had disappeared. She followed a little way behind. Mead was extending the paving out from under the verandah. He was digging holes and placing into the ground the rocks he had split from the granite. He was fitting them together as though they were shapes from a puzzle.

'What's Isaac doing?' asked Anderson.

Mead looked up and would have shrugged nonchalantly except that he saw the look on Anderson's face. Instead he stood tall and looked nervously about him.

'I don't know. He was here. I didn't give him much attention.'

Dorothea walked behind Anderson and under the verandah to the doorway that led into the kitchen. Church looked up from the table. His thin black beard made his face seem even longer.

'What's wrong?' he asked.

'Isaac has taken Jack's gun.'

Church's glance flicked through the doorway to where Anderson leant against a post talking to Mead. He looked back at Dorothea with a frown, pulling his eyebrows together. They knew Isaac. There might be nothing in it. But if he was in one of his moods, he was just as likely to shoot them all. She suddenly wondered where the black women were. They wouldn't be far for although Sal's leg had healed she still had trouble walking. And then Dorothea thought of her sister. She should warn her.

⌢

They all gathered in the hut, mostly pretending they weren't worried at all. But when the wind moved the bough of a tree against the wall, they looked up. Mary and Matthew were with Church around the table. Mead and Anderson were just inside the doorway. Dorothea made everyone tea. There was no sign of Dinah and the others. It reminded her of when their mother had begun to drink. Everyone would fix their faces in expressions of unconcern but they were unable to control the number of times they looked to the door. Except Father. He would yell at them to stop the boy from crying. Then William would cry louder. And their mother would return like a creature from the forest. Her shawl would be damp and smell sweet and sickly of spirit. It would fall over one shoulder, and her boots would trip over the ends. Then Father would take over. And her bruises would hardly have faded before she was gone again. Dorothea couldn't remember her mother drinking when they lived in England

She knew her mother had been disappointed. They all were. It had been a long voyage. They had berths in steerage, separate from the handful of saloon passengers travelling with the governor of the new colony, Captain Stirling. Men with capital, who would walk the upper deck, smoking their pipes, wearing black dress suits. They would be the new aristocracy of the small colony. Her family had nothing when they arrived. They were no different from the natives who wandered amongst the houses asking for flour and biscuit. It was that her mother couldn't live with.

She wondered whether her mother knew the *Mountaineer* had run aground or whether she imagined they were living their new lives in Van Diemen's Land. Of course she wouldn't have expected to hear from them and there were four other children to concern her. But who would have thought that it could have ended like this? Dorothea looked around. The hut was like a dim dusty cave. Skins hanging from the walls prevented the light shining through the timber. The hearth glowed orange and smoked.

She lifted the tea to her mouth, and she swallowed, breathing the sharp fragrance in the steam, no sweetener any more, just strong and black. She moved her chair away from the smoke. As it scraped across the rock they looked towards her and then turned away. Except Anderson who held her gaze with his. But then sticks were broken as heavy feet stepped on them outside on the path. Anderson turned into the doorway, his bulk filling the frame. They couldn't see past him. Then they heard Isaac's voice.

'Give them black crows a bit of a fright.'

There was silence.

'Aww Jack … why you looking like that?' he spoke with a whine in his voice. 'Here, you can have it. There ain't no shot in it anyways.'

Anderson took the gun and retreated into his room. Isaac stepped through the doorway and looked around, grinning.

'Right little gathering in here.' He nodded towards Dorothea. 'Make us a tea.'

After a while he left again.

⌒

Church and Matthew resumed their conversation.

'It's in a gully behind the ti-tree,' said Matthew.

'What?' asked Dorothea.

'A grave,' replied Church. 'There's a copper plate over the top of it.'

'What does it say?'

'Douglas, 1803.'

'Whereabouts? Copper'd be useful,' said Mead.

'You can't disturb someone's grave,' said Church, frowning. 'That's a sacrilege.'

'That's what?' said Mead. 'Poor bastard don't know, do he?'

'If I were to perish on this island, I would like for the sake of my family to have my grave marked.'

'Ain't got no family,' said Mead. 'Last I heard anyways. But that's not accounting for the gin I had on Preservation.'

Matthew looked at his wife and then around at the others. 'When you're dead, you're dead. I'll promise you though,' he said to Church, 'if you pop your clogs, I'll bury you with a few stones and a cross on top.' He grinned. 'But if you want something written, you better do it now 'cause there ain't anyone here who can write.'

'Jack can,' said Dorothea.

They all looked at her.

'What would you write?' asked Mead, ignoring her, his eyes scrunched at the corners. 'Here lies a swell's son run out.'

He chuckled into his beard and wiped the spit from the corner of his mouth. Something crossed Church's face. Regret, perhaps. She thought he looked closer to death than the rest of them. While the faces around the table were like hardened leather, including her sister and, she supposed, hers as well, he had remained pale. He had stayed indoors most of the time and he always wore his black beaver hat.

'Can you talk about something else,' muttered Mary.

After a short silence Mead began one of his stories of chasing sperm whales across the Pacific, explaining that he was like a cat with nine lives. Dorothea remembered an earlier version of his yarn and left to get some salted meat from the storeroom.

In the evening she sat with Anderson under the verandah looking out over the clearing. They hadn't seen Isaac for dinner and she didn't dare ask after him. The upper branches and the trunk of the eucalypt glowed white with the light from the weak golden sun that disappeared behind the dune. The night air drew around them like a damp blanket. Frogs chorused, their numbers having increased considerably with all the rain. But tonight the sky had cleared. And the first star appeared against the pale purple backdrop and hung between the leaves of the two trees. Voices murmured through the open doorway. Anderson sighed and her eyes traced his heavy profile as he stared ahead. Then he turned and asked what she wanted.

She looked down at her hands that were never clean. They were working hands. Her nails striped black and the knuckles worn and peeling. She turned them over. Her palms were worse, reddened and blistered. The lines strongly defined. What did she want? She knew she wanted to leave the island. Since she had known that they didn't have to wait for a trader, she had become more and more anxious to fly over the crest of the wave, to go against the swell rather than to have it roll towards her every day. Only then would she be able to breathe freely, to expand her heart.

And what of him? She kept her eyes down as she cleaned the dirt from under one fingernail with another. She would like to see him in fine clothes. Tight pantaloons and a twilled cotton shirt, the collar held in place with a stock of the finest silk, and a waistcoat and coat of camelot. He could take her arm and they would walk between the houses, past the Sherratt Family Inn, up the road that wound towards the hill. And she would show him into her family's home and they would admire his dress, her gentleman of means.

The sea surged onto the sand and then thundered as the line of the wave broke further along the beach. The action at one end triggering the foam to fold into itself all the way around to the other end. Even though the sand and the bush that grew like the hair on a young man's face hid the waves from view, she knew how it would be.

January 1886

The sealer Billy Andrews looked after my baby and I. He gave my child his name. He knew how Jack died. He had stolen from Jack before. Sometimes we lived on Michaelmas Island, which wasn't far from the Sound. Then one day he went to sea and he didn't come back either.

King George Sound 1835, James Manning

He couldn't remember when his tongue began to feel like a lump of dry meat in his mouth. At least he didn't have to listen to Jem whining any more because he couldn't talk either. He realised then that he couldn't hear him at all. Slowly he turned. Any movement was an effort. Just to turn his neck to the side. It was alright when he walked slowly in a straight line. Then he didn't have to think and he could put one foot in front of the other. He panted and stumbled, his trouser leg catching on the sharp spike of a branch. Jem's body lay curled into the rock. He reached down towards him, opening his mouth to urge him on. But he had no words. All he could utter was a hoarse cry. It was enough to make him start.

Manning looked into a face of raw tight skin and eyes without hope.

He half pulled and helped him up. They stood leaning against each other, panting. The effort caused everything to shimmer before him. A black shadow crossed in front of him and slipped into a tree. The tree came towards him and he crumpled. They collapsed together, folded one across the other. He lay on his back, his neck tilted behind Jem's shoulder. When his eyes opened, they held only the sky. Had he died?

Jem lay beneath him without moving. But he sensed the movement of others. Shapes of people. They were red. A man leant over him and he smelt a strange combination of smoke and an animal in semi-decay. He wore a dog's tail in his hair. His face was shiny with red pigment and his eyes were big and round. He turned and spoke over his shoulder to the others. Manning couldn't understand him. And he didn't care. If this was the way it was to be he was glad for it had been too hard. He closed his eyes, wanting it to be over quickly.

'Enoc eean?' *What is your name?*

The man grasped his hand as though to shake it. He felt Jem stir beneath him. He struggled to get up but managed only to slide off Jem. They both sat on the ground, holding onto their knees for support. Four men who bristled with spears surrounded them. Manning tried to speak. His eyes imploring the one who had spoken to understand.

'E Naaw?' *What, What do you say?*

The talkative one grinned and turned back to his companions. They all laughed and began to move away. Manning struggled trying to lift himself up with his good arm. They hesitated, watching him. Jem moaned and laid his head on his knees. Manning gestured with his hand to show that they needed to eat. He made signals that they were hungry and thirsty, that they had walked a long, long way and that they must go further.

'Ahhh,' said the man who had turned away.

He nodded as though he understood. He talked to the others and then suddenly broke into a chant. But they slipped between two bushes and disappeared. That was it then. Manning lay back on the rock to wait for the darkness to begin. He had nothing left: no reserves from which to draw. Jem had slumped forward, his head almost touching the rock, and then gradually he fell sideways.

Sometime later, it could have been that day, the next day or the day after, the men returned. Manning's eyes had crusted shut and he opened them with difficulty. They brought with them whale meat and water. They squatted, feeding them small pieces of blubber and pouring water from bark into their mouths.

'Ca,' one of them said to Manning and helped him to his feet.

The others lifted Jem and supported him. They carried them away from the sea, light filtered by leaves flickering at the edge of their vision, into more densely wooded country. Smells changed and became richer and more pungent and peppery. A dampness came up from the ground.

It seemed a long time but it may not have been. The forest cleared and a river lay before them. On the other side rust-coloured rushes and the white twisted stems of the paperbark were mirrored in the still water. Further along an island of granite stones dusted with gold lichen and streaked white with pelican droppings lay in the middle. Birds glided across their reflection. White cockatoos flew overhead and landed amongst the treetops, chattering and shrill with their squabbles and squawks. He smelt a campfire. They veered away from the river and beneath the rivergums there were people. Their homes were a few sticks stuck in the ground, bent over like bows and thatched with the leaves of a grasstree. There were four of them and each had a fire smoking in front of it. Women and children and a couple of old men wrapped in kangaroo-skin cloaks huddled over the embers. They remained where they were as the men brought Manning and Jem into the clearing.

A child leapt up and two dogs came forward to sniff their heels. Then the excitement started and it was impossible to tell who was talking. Manning was too tired to care. He reached for Jem's shoulder and the pair stumbled across to the closest campfire and collapsed beside it. The noise continued around them. Occasionally faces that were friendly peered into theirs. And then later when it got darker, cooked meat on sticks was pushed into their hands. The smell almost made Manning faint. Gingerly he sucked the hot meat. Finally when he placed it into his mouth, he realised he didn't have the strength to chew it. He looked at Jem who was having the same problem. He leant into Jem and closed his eyes.

When he woke, the leaves above were etched in gold light and the crows had begun their chorus. Two men and a dog lay in the shelter behind them. He thought Jem was dead until he poked him and he moved. Two women were on the other side of the clearing. When they noticed he was awake, they grinned shyly. They were grinding a substance between two flat stones and working it into a paste. They roasted it on their fire. Then the younger of the two carried it over on a piece of bark. It tasted like nutty bread. Manning swallowed it all, quickly before Jem was properly awake. But he needn't have worried for they made some more and shared it with both of them.

He could feel his head clearing but when he turned to speak to Jem he found his voice had not yet returned. But it seemed that his ability to focus had. For when he looked around he saw everything. Glassy water like a mirror flickered through the gap in the trees. He made his way towards it and knelt in its icy shallows. It reflected his face and his hair. It wasn't someone he knew. He cupped the soft water and washed the salty grime from his face and swallowed deeply. Jem shuffled to the water's edge.

'Those hills, I know them,' he croaked.

Manning looked to the purple mounds in the distance. The river wound around and thickened towards them. Could it be possible that they weren't far from the Sound? He didn't dare believe it. But his blood seemed to pump with more energy and he straightened without difficulty. They returned to the camp amidst the curious stares of their hosts. A man they hadn't seen before came towards them. He had worsted yarn made from some sort of fur wrapped around his waist, head and left arm. His hair was bound round the back of his head and decorated with feathers. His skin was painted a brick-dust colour. He was tall and handsome.

'Waiter,' he said. Indicating that that was his name.

They gave him their names. And he repeated them slowly with a strange accent.

'You go to white people?' And he gestured northeast.

'Yes,' nodded Manning. 'To King George Sound, can you lead us there?'

Jem nodded too. Waiter nodded and the others who had gathered to watch their exchange moved their heads up and down with great exaggeration and amusement. Manning half smiled and looked to Jem. He shrugged. But it seemed that Waiter had understood them. For he was speaking sharply to the others. And people began to move in all directions.

⁓

But when they set out there was just Waiter and another who came with them. They headed further inland until the river narrowed and they were able to cross it. The current was strong and it ripped around their chests. Manning checked behind to see how Jem was faring. Although unsteady, he was pushing his way through to the shallower water. It wasn't long afterwards that they came to another river which was salty. Jem seemed excited by the sight of it winding towards a large lake flanked by hazy hills. Manning couldn't help but feel it too. Although he wasn't sure whether it meant they would be there that night or the next week.

Crossing that river was harder. Their feet sunk deep into the mud and it took every effort to lift one foot at a time. It swirled around them at waist height so that when they reached the other side they lay on its grassy bank, gasping for breath. Waiter and his companion watched them with concern. Waiter took out from beneath his skin cloak the glowing cone of a banksia flower and kindled a small fire. They dug out the root of the reed that grew at the water's edge and crushed it into a paste then roasted it on the fire. Breaking off chunks they shared it with Manning and Jem. The day, which had begun brightly, turned dull, and the air, although it had lost its chill, smelt of rain.

They began again although Manning and Jem trailed heavily behind the agile steps of their guides. Manning suddenly realised that they were following a well-worn trail and then he noticed fresh horse droppings and prints in the sand. Surely they would reach the settlement by evening. Had he not thought that he probably wouldn't have been able to go on. But the excitement drove him further and he found strength he didn't realise he had. He could see that Jem was suffering too. But he would not stop; they could not stop now.

When it began to rain heavily the natives took them to John Henty's property. There was a hut there and a man who worked for Henty. It was where the river drained into Oyster Harbour. After they were given hot watery stew, they were wrapped in blankets and left to sleep by the fire. Although Manning had heard that the settlement of King George Sound was on a harbour, Jem explained that it wasn't Oyster Harbour.

'There are two harbours,' he said. 'Princess Royal Harbour is where the town is and that's to the west of the Sound.'

'So how far?' murmured Manning, his voice muffled by blankets.

'Four hours, maybe.'

Waiter and his friend led them into the settlement. Houses were built on a slope that continued down to a sandy shore. They stood at the top of the rise between the two hills, Mount Melville and Mount Clarence, and saw beyond the buildings the land-locked harbour stretching out before them. It was oval shaped and behind its far shore was the continuation of the coastline in the form of a headland high and striped with gullies so that it looked as though it were cloaked by lumpy green and grey fabric. And looking back towards the east was the Sound with two big scrubby islands at its mouth. A smallish boat passed through the narrow channel from the Sound and into the harbour in front of them. They looked like sealers and Manning wondered where Anderson was.

The two natives walked on ahead along the road that curved down the side of Mount Clarence. But Manning and Jem remained where they were, unable to move. Both overcome by the journey's end but for different reasons. A curtain of water engulfed them and the little whitewashed houses blurred in the rain. The place seemed deserted. Manning was thinking of how long it had been and how hard. Rain ran down the back of his neck and under his skin cloak and watered down the salt from his eyes.

A native appeared from between two houses further down the hill. There was whoop and a yell and Waiter and his friend were surrounded by the emotional greetings of the King George Sound natives. It attracted the attention of others and people left their houses and looked up towards Manning and Jem. The rain eased and they trod through the mud, stepping over small streams of water that carved gullies in the road to greet them. Jem seemed to recognise some of them and he described briefly what had happened to them, clearly invigorated by their interest. While they talked Manning kept looking down at the settlement, stunned at how small it was. There were a couple of two-storey brick buildings but mostly they were small wattle and daub houses thatched with reeds. Streets were merely thin scars through the bush. His attention returned to Jem who was telling their story and saying that their hope had been to get to the mainland where they knew they were safe from the rogue who had stolen all his friend's money.

'And your sisters are still there?' cried a woman.

Jem nodded slowly.

'You best report it.'

'To the magistrate,' said another.

Manning watched Jem and then he said to him, 'Come on. Let's get out of the rain.'

The small group parted and allowed them to continue. They left the natives on the side of the hill. Instead of taking the road into the settlement, they turned off onto a track. It took them up and around the northwestern side of Mount Clarence. From there they were unable to see the settlement.

They came to a timber shack surrounded by thickly wooded bush. A young girl tossed a pail of water from the open doorway. She looked up.

'Ma! Ma! Someone's here.' She stood with her back against the doorway, peering out into the drizzle. Her mother came to her side.

'It's me, Ma. Jem,' he said weakly, when he got closer.

'My God, so it is.' She wiped her hands on her skirt and came towards them. Her eyes, sunk into a red fleshy face, blinked rapidly. She cupped his face in her hands and peered into it, not recognising the boy who had left her just six months earlier.

They were brought inside and taken into the kitchen. They huddled over the hearth. Jem's mother sent the girl, Caroline, to Cheynes for liquor. Jem had another sister Netty. When she leant across to reach the pot in the fireplace, her ripe breasts strained at the low neckline of her gown. But she glared at Manning when she caught him staring. Still he found it difficult to keep his eyes off her for she was young and clean. His eyes narrowed as they followed her out the door.

Jem exhausted himself explaining what had happened. The questions kept coming but after a while they couldn't be bothered to answer them. When Caroline returned she had with her a young boy, William, who must have been about seven. He was a thin pale lad with blond curls and large brown eyes that followed his brother whenever he moved or spoke. The mother told Jem that his father and another brother Charlie were away on the other side of the harbour, felling timber.

The rum lit a warm place in Manning's belly. It took away the disappointment and smoothed the edge of his pain. Netty brought them blankets. They lay by the fire. And slept that day and into the night. Manning waking when the fire was like the glowing eyes of a wild thing. He could hear the whispered words and giggles of women. It stirred him and he decided he wanted the chance to have what other men had.

When they stood before the magistrate the next day, Manning almost couldn't do it. He realised then that it was a capital offence. That Anderson would hang for it or at the very least be transported to Port Arthur. Then he remembered what Anderson had forced him to do and how his woman had looked at him as if he were dirt.

He watched the bent head of the man as he scratched the words on paper. He looked up and Manning recoiled slightly from his severely scarred face. Perhaps he should have asked about a passage to the Swan River settlement instead. His eyes were drawn to the raised lump of scar tissue that glowed white and cut the face in half and he wondered what had happened to him. Sir Richard Spencer glared from his good eye.

'I shall read you my letter to the Colonial Secretary's Office. Please correct me if I am in error.'

He cleared his throat, stated the day's date and began:

Sir, I have the honour to acquaint you for the information of His Excellency that two lads (James Newell and James Manning) reached the settlement yesterday, who were landed on the mainland, opposite Middle Island, on the 23rd June last. They are reduced almost to skeletons and have nearly lost their voice. I am delighted to add that the moment the natives (the White Cockatoo, Murray and Hill men tribes) fell in with them, that they were nursed, fed and almost carried to Mr John Hentys. I have requested Mr Browne to issue a small portion of flour to each native and a duck frock each, to two, who were most active and kind to them on their journey. I will also issue one week's rations to the two lads, and a duck frock to each of them. The Gentlemen in the settlement have been very liberal in subscribing to buy the poor fellows blankets and cloaths. A bag of rice and sugar has also been issued to give all the natives a supper. When the men are sufficiently recovered I shall take their Declarations of what has happened to them and enclose it with this.

He looked up but Manning had only heard him say it was the tenth day of August 1835. What a lot of time he had wasted.

January 1886

The light is growing dim. It is as though someone is drawing the curtains. Soon they will meet in the middle. Sometimes I hear the sea inside my head. The way it would roar on the southern side of the island. If only we had known what was before us. Then we would have known we were safe. We had everything but we thought it was nothing. I want to go somewhere warm and quiet, where the light is soft like a summer sunset.

King George Sound 1835, Dorothea Newell

Dorothea stood on the shore of the Princess Royal Harbour, her skins wrapped tightly around her. Looking up the hill to where they had all gone. It was late afternoon and it felt as though her life was over. They had even taken his whaleboat. But he had fought them. She had seen her brother and his friend in the crowd of people who had come to watch them arrest Anderson and Isaac when they hauled up on the sand. She had thought at first that they were merchants who had come to buy the skins.

She turned her back on the settlement and looked out over the harbour. It was a smooth layer of glass until some unseen force rippled its surface. A ship sat out in the middle, its masts stripped bare. They had sailed, all of them, between the rocks that marked the entrance to the harbour from the deep dark water of the Sound. She could see the hazy outline of Breaksea Island and the island beside it, Michaelmas. They had passed through the north channel only a few hours earlier. She thought of the black women back on Bald Island, some twenty miles to the east. What would happen to them if Anderson didn't return?

She felt like a shell washed up on the beach. What was inside had died. It was hard to remember how she had felt when she saw the mouth of the Sound. How elated they had been that they had survived. Mary had almost forgotten she wasn't speaking to her for she looked over her shoulder and smiled. Dorothea had thought then that everything would be alright.

It had taken them about three weeks to sail from Middle Island. God, how she regretted forcing Anderson to take them back. The fine days had come early. And the winds had turned favourable. They loaded the whaleboat so high that it sat low in the water. That was why it took so long. Anderson had to leave some skins behind. They kept close to the coast and in the lee of islands, exposed to the full force of the swell as little as possible. For most of the journey the weather was perfect and they had sailed with a brisk breeze from the east.

They had reached Bald Island three days earlier. They set up camp, erecting the tent they had brought. A small squall delayed their departure by a day and Anderson decided to unload some of the boat's contents. He left there the tent, the pots and their bedding and the black women to look after everything.

But before then, before they hauled up on Bald Island, she remembered. The hard, tight skin of his arms around her, leaning into him, as they drifted on a sea that sparkled like a carpet of silver. The men laid their oars down. They were amongst islands of freckled granite with smooth steep edges washed white by the swell. A sea haze hung between them. Spray spouted above small rocks that broke the surface and around them churned white-laced foam over pale green ripples. Dark slippery seals ducked and weaved through the water. It felt then as though they were suspended in time but she knew it was just an illusion for she could feel the current beneath the boat as it bore them along. The sun lay warmth over them and they were carried towards an island in the shape of a figure of eight where they would spend the night.

The sun had sunk behind the hill and the settlement was in shadow. The air chilled her. She couldn't keep standing here on the sand. A little way to her left was the pub, a two-storey timber place, painted green. She couldn't go there either. Its doors opened and someone fell out. He scrambled upright and stumbled towards her. Before she could move, he spat at her feet. She left then and hurried through the peppermint trees and across to the road that led up the side of the hill. Conscious of people in doorways and someone with a wheelbarrow but she kept her eyes on the dirt.

By the time she reached the top of the rise it was dark. The yellow light winked through the bushes ahead. She stumbled over the rocks on the track. They were all there: her father, mother, brothers and sisters, Matthew and Manning. She was greeted with silence. But no one told her to go. She went into the kitchen and her brother William, who was playing by the fire, smiled widely, wrapping his arms around her legs. It was too much then and she sunk to the floor and cried. Her mother followed her into the room. She took the pot from the fire and spooned out a bowl of stew. As she gave it to her she took her hand and brought it to the bowl. When Dorothea grasped it, her mother smoothed the hair from her daughter's eyes. Then she left to join the others.

Dorothea stayed by the fire with William chattering around her. He asked her many questions and she tried to answer them. But her thoughts got in the way. Eventually he grew tired and lay with his head on her knee. She looked down at his sleeping face, his soft skin and the delicate curve of his lashes. She was glad to see him.

She lifted his head gently onto the crook of her arm and curled into his warm, slight body and slept.

She didn't go far from the fire the next day and the day after. People came and went. She didn't want to know anything. There were visitors, people wanting to hear what had happened to them. But if they caught sight of her they looked at her strangely. She knew she looked a mess. Her hair had grown into wild irregular lengths. And she kept her seal-skin coat wrapped firmly around her. After they left, her mother would walk unsteadily into the kitchen and sit on the stool, her back against the wall. Her mouth would slacken and she'd slip into a noisy sleep.

William kept her from thinking. He took her up to the steep rise behind the hut and into the bush where black cockatoos crawled over the red bottlebrush tree, ripping the heart of the flower and tearing strips from the bark with their strong curved beaks. They would peer sideways with eyes that saw everything.

She was there when Caroline called. There was someone for her at the door. Police Constable Dunn. He announced that she was required to give evidence tomorrow. It was as though small spiders crawled down the nape of her neck.

She woke in the night, cold. The fire had gone out. She set about finding more wood. It was usually by the door. But tonight there was none. Outside, the darkness was heavy and she stumbled towards the woodpile. She could see a light down the hill and to her right. That was Spencer's farm, Sir Richard Spencer whom she would have to speak to in the morning. She wondered where they had put him. And Isaac too. For they had both been charged. She had been told to go to the old commandant's residence on Parade Street. Perhaps they were in the old gaol. She didn't think it had been used since the settlement was an outpost for New South Wales convicts.

When the dark sky brightened she walked alone down the hill. There were two ships in the harbour, sitting like old ducks on still water. And the shoreline was dotted with small craft coming and going, ripples stretching wide in their wake. She wore her tammar-skin shoes but she had borrowed her mother's dark brown gown. She had straightened her hair with oil and had parted it in the middle, holding it in place with combs behind her ears. She shivered for she was without her seal skin.

She reached the ballast brick house of George Cheyne and turned right following the road to the creek that cut the little town in half. Timber planks had been placed across it.

No one had asked her what she was going to say. But their unspoken words had hung heavy. She walked along the thin planking but her feet got wet at the other end when she stepped off into the mud.

The street was wide and dirty. On either side of it there was bush and then occasionally, where it had been cleared, a small cottage. Some were half finished: a whitewashed wall standing alone and sticks of wattle strung together in bundles. She reached the end of the street and turned up towards the old commandant's residence, a shabby grey building enclosed by a brush fence. She noticed a group of people standing in a half-circle. She could see the wooden door to the house. She would be able to slip inside without them noticing her. As she was about to enter she glanced up and saw between two people. They were gathered around Anderson. He was in stocks. His head bowed by the wooden restraint, his big hands useless.

She grasped the side of the wall for support. His head lifted slightly and he saw her. In that moment she saw everything: the anger, the shame, the defeat and the injustice. She looked at the big solid door in front of her and she pulled it open. Three men sat at a long table at the other end of the room. In the middle was Sir Richard Spencer. On his left she recognised Captain Peter Belches, and on the other side Captain Alexander Cheyne, for they were both men who had come out on the *James Pattison*. She stood just inside the door, hesitant at first and then she took a deep breath, lifted her head and walked tall towards the row of seating facing the men.

⌒

Afterwards she knew what she had done was right. But it was no comfort. Not when she was to go home and look into the faces of her family. So she stayed down by the water's edge, watching the clouds clear and the colours deepen. She overheard men who were waiting at the landing stage for flour to be taken out to one of the ships. The ship was taking female convicts to Sydney. It had been damaged in a storm and had called in for repairs. There was no sign of life on its decks for clearly the women were being kept below.

When she did go back to the house there was no need to say anything. Jem and Manning weren't around. And Mary and Matthew had gone to enquire about a passage to Sydney. She wondered how they felt. Knowing that Jack's life was in their hands. She had told the three men the truth. That she had gone to live with Jack after three weeks. Now everyone would know. But what did it matter?

She sat on the step at the front of the hut. There she could see the purple ranges in the distance. She heard there were grassy plains at the foothills and that men had taken sheep to them. Already she felt as though a part of her life had ended. She almost couldn't remember what the island was like. And although she had caught a glimpse of him that morning, the memory of his face, his eyes, his mouth was fading. The way his lips moved when he spoke her name.

~

She sat quietly in the corner while everyone ate together. She found it impossible to swallow. Manning had said that a decision would be made in the morning. And he would be arranging his passage to the Swan River. She noticed his quick glance towards Netty when he spoke. She was pleased to see that he was ignored.

The next morning she looked for her mother and found her at the back of the house sitting on a tree stump. She could see that she wasn't well. She seemed hollow, as though what life she had in her was leaking out. For as long as she could remember her mother's hair had been grey. It was wrapped around the back of her head but listless strands hung about her face. And beneath her eyes lay dark shadows. She looked up when she saw her daughter. Dorothea came and sat opposite her on the fallen trunk of a tree.

After a while she said: 'They had him in stocks.'

'He's a bad man.'

'He ain't, Ma. He ain't a bad person.'

Her mother sighed and she shook her head wearily.

'A black man is a bad man. Whether he is or not.'

So when Anderson appeared around the side of the house they both stared at him, speechless. He stood in front of the sun, a featureless black man against the white light of day. But when she got closer she saw it was him. Even though she spoke the truth, she hadn't expected the three men to listen. He told them it was Mead's evidence as well that had made them realise it was impossible to prove that he and Isaac had stolen forty-six pounds from Manning. The trial would not go ahead. She smiled and the air left her lungs easily. She glanced at her mother and read in her eyes a warning but she took no notice. She brought him food. And he ate outside under the tree.

Later they walked down the hill as the sun was setting behind them. He led her to the pub on the waterfront where he had taken a room. His whaleboat had been restored to him. Mead and Isaac had sold the skins and bought new supplies to take back with them. They would camp beside the boat that night and leave before dawn. Jack was worried about the black women.

There were about twenty people around the bar, mostly mariners. She liked the fact that when she entered with Jack they looked away. One of them didn't for it was Church, who was seated away from everyone else by the window. She met his gaze and smiled at him for she felt strangely pleased to see him. Anderson was facing the bar when Church got up and came towards her. He didn't look any different. He still wore his black coat but perhaps his hair and his beard had been trimmed.

'What are you doing here?' she asked, smiling.

'Waiting for another vessel,' he said, and he looked towards the window and in the direction of the sea. He shrugged his thin shoulders. 'There is no place for me in this wilderness.'

'But where will you go?'

'I'm returning to England, to my brother and his wife,' he said as he turned back to her, his eyes inscrutable.

Anderson looked over his shoulder at Church and acknowledged him with a nod. Church raised his hat and moved towards the door. Then he was gone and she wondered where he had got the money for his passage. She realised too that she had never felt as far from England as she did now.

~

The bar was nearly empty when she looked intently at Anderson.

'I want to come with you,' she said.

He studied her face. After a while he spoke, shaking his head slightly: 'No, you don't.'

She didn't say anything. But the next day when it was time to push off from the shore and the light beneath the land cast a weak path to the east, she was standing beside him.

22 January 1886

The minister came today. He asked after George. I didn't say that I hadn't seen him. He wanted to know if I was reading my Bible. After he left, I looked inside the cover. 18th January 1837, Dorothea Anderson. It cost me four shillings from Hugh Spencer who drowned, I think. I bought it because I wanted to know what Jack knew. That was the year our daughter was born.

Was Matthew there when you died? I hope he held your hand. Jack is close to me now. I can smell him. It is like the rich scent of a seal. I know I will see you soon. And that you have forgiven me.

Afterword

Dorothea died on 22 January 1886. Her passing was noted by Kate Keyser, a resident of King George Sound (Albany), Western Australia, from 1837 to 1886. She wrote in her diary: *Old Dolly Pettit died today. A woman of property and yet it is said she died of neglect and starvation. Poor old thing she had no children to care for her.*

Most of the events that occurred in the life of Dorothea Newell, or Dolly Pettit as she later became known, are true. Dorothea came out from England with her family to King George Sound in the early 1830s and died there in 1886.

The people mentioned in her story are also true. Their characters, however, are my own invention and in some cases I have created their backgrounds. The inspiration for the story was drawn from Western Australia's Records of the Colonial Secretary's Office, 1 August–30 September 1835 and from the Albany Court House Records 1834–1841.

The house where Dorothea died is now a popular restaurant in Albany. When this book was almost completed, I spoke to its current owners. They were unaware of the early history of the house. They claim it is haunted by a small grey-haired woman who sits by the fireplace in one of the front rooms and by a man who comes up from the sea and walks around the house to keep her safe.

A note on characters and sources

References to the Newell family can be found in the *Dictionary of Western Australians 1829–1850; Volume 1: Early Settlers*, published by the University of Western Australia Press. An outline of Dorothea's experience on Middle Island was recorded in her deposition at Anderson's trial (*Albany Court House Records 1834–1841*). What happened to her after Middle Island has been pieced together from snippets of fact and hearsay recorded in newspaper articles and other documents collected by the Local Studies Section of the Albany Library. However, her time in England and that of her family's was my own invention. It is also generally believed that her father came to Australia as a New South Wales convict. Descendants of the family believe otherwise, however, and think that James Newell senior was mistaken for someone else. I am convinced that there is sufficient evidence to support their view. I have remained true to what is generally thought to have been the fates of all the Newell family members.

John Anderson, or Black Jack Anderson, the African-American, has been mentioned in Australian historical texts on sealing and Kangaroo Island. He is recorded as appearing in the 1830s, possibly as a deserter off an American whaler. Little else is known about him. He and Isaac Winterbourne were charged with the theft from James Manning of forty-six pounds. They were acquitted due to lack of evidence. Anderson was also charged over altercations with the sealer William Andrews. Anderson, in his defence, claimed that Andrews had robbed him of a variety of items, including two native women. On 29 March 1837 Robert Gamble reported Anderson's death in a statement made to Patrick Taylor, Justice of the Peace at Albany.

The names of the two Aboriginal women with Anderson and the one Aboriginal woman with Isaac on Middle Island are unknown. A native woman was apparently killed with Anderson on Mondrain Island.

The conversation between Mead, Church and Matthew about a copper plaque on page 190 refers to an actual historical event. Charles Douglas was Matthew Flinders' boatswain. As the HMS *Investigator* approached Middle Island on 18 May 1803 Douglas died of dysentery. He was buried on the island and an inscription upon copper was placed over his grave. Until now this copper plaque has never been found.

The circumstances in which James Manning found himself on Middle Island are true. However, he was a passenger on the *Defiance* and not a crew member. The crew, who set off back to Sydney in a longboat after the *Defiance* was wrecked, was in fact never heard of again. Anderson accused Manning of stealing but it wasn't from Owens. It was from George Merredith, the captain of the *Defiance*, while they were all on Kangaroo Island. Manning and Jem Newell were left by Anderson to walk from the mainland near Middle Island to Albany. The letter on page 205 is an edited copy of the original letter written by Sir Richard Spencer, Resident Magistrate of Albany, to the Colonial Secretary's Office. I have been unable to discover what happened to James Manning but it appears that he never reached the Swan River colony. If he did, there is no official record of it.

Mary Newell married Matthew Gill, by then a servant of Sir Richard Spencer, on 8 September 1834. A Mary Gill was buried in Sydney on 25 March 1840. She was twenty-eight years old.

The other people named in the story — Owens, John White (Johno) the boy James (Jimmy) and Francis Mead, as well as Isaac and Anderson — were officially recorded as being on the island at the time. Evanson Jansen and his crew and passengers landed on Middle Island after the *Mountaineer* was wrecked at Thistle Cove, near Esperance.

For this story to be authentic in its descriptions of the sealers and the experiences of early colonists such as the Newell family, I have drawn on the following sources:

A Charles Begg and Neil C Begg, *The World of John Boultbee Including an Account of Sealing in Australia and New Zealand*; W Jeffrey Bolster, *Black Jacks, African American Seamen in the Age of Sail*; Don Brown, 'Black Whalers, They Were Great While it Lasted' in *American Visions*, 1987, October, 26–30; WA Cawthorne, *The Kangaroo Islanders, A Story of South Australia before Colonisation*; Phillip A Clarke, 'Early European Interaction with Aboriginal Hunters and Gatherers on Kangaroo Island, South Australia' in *Aboriginal History*, 1996, 20, 51–81; JS Cumpston, *First Visitors to Bass Strait*; JS Cumpston, *Kangaroo Island*; Paul Edwards and Edward Dabydeen (ed), *Black Writers in Britain 1760–1890*; Tatania de Fircks, 'Costume in the Early Years of Western Australia' in

Journal and Proceedings of the Royal Western Australian Historical Society, vol 9, part 6, 1988, 27–38; Tim Flannery (ed), *John Nicol, Mariner, Life and Adventures, 1776–1801*; Donald Garden, *Albany, A Panorama of the Sound from 1827*; BK de Garis (ed), *Portraits of the South-West Aborigines, Women and the Environment*; Neville Green (ed), *Nyungar—The People, Aboriginal Customs in the South West of Australia*; Pamela Horn, *The Rural World 1780–1850, Social Change in the English Countryside*; Lawrence C Howard, 'A Note on New England Whaling and Africa before 1860' in *Negro History Bulletin*, 1858, 13–15; Jorgen Jorgenson, *Jorgen Jorgenson's Observations on Pacific Trade and Sealing and Whaling in Australian and New Zealand Waters before 1805*; Leon F Litwack, *North of Slavery, The Negro in the Free States 1790–1860*; GA Mawer, *Ahab's Trade, The Saga of South Seas Whaling*; N Plomley and K Henley, 'The Sealers of Bass Strait and the Cape Barren Community' in *Papers and Proceedings of the Tasmanian Historical Research Association*, vol 37, 1990, 37–127; Nathaniel Philbrick, *In the Heart of the Sea*; Rosemary Ransom, *Taraba, Tasmanian Aboriginal Stories* (DECCD); John Rintoul, *Esperance Yesterday and Today*; Winnis J Ruediger, *Border's Land Kangaroo Island 1802–1836*; Lyndall Ryan, *The Aboriginal Tasmanians*; Iain Stuart, 'Sea Rats, Bandits and Roistering Buccaneers, What Were the Bass Strait Sealers Really Like?' in the *Journal of the Royal Australian Historical Society*, 1997, 83(1), 47–58; Vernon Williams, *The Straitsmen, A Romance*; Guy Wright, *Sons and Seals*.

Skins

SARAH HAY was born in Esperance, Western Australia, in 1966. A journalist and public relations consultant, she began her career as a cadet livestock reporter in Perth. She has worked in England as a reporter for a national newspaper. She has also been a writer for two public relations firms in Perth. Currently an undergraduate at the University of Western Australia, she is completing a Bachelor of Arts in English and Philosophy and writing her second novel. She lives in Perth with her husband and son.

SARAH HAY

ALLEN&UNWIN

First published in 2002

This project has been assisted by the Commonwealth
Government through the Australia Council, its arts funding
and advisory body.

Allen & Unwin
83 Alexander Street
Crows Nest NSW 2065
Australia
Phone: (61 2) 8425 0100
Fax: (61 2) 9906 2218
Email: info@allenandunwin.com
Web: www.allenandunwin.com

National Library of Australia
Cataloguing-in-Publication entry:

Hay, Sarah, 1966–.
    Skins.

    ISBN 1 86508 807 2.

    1. Aborigines, Australian—Women—Western Australia—History.
    2. Sealers (Persons)—Western Australia—History.
    3. Aborigines, Australian—Western Australia—History. I. Title.

305.4889915

Set in 11.5pt on 14pt Adobe Garamond by Asset Typesetting Pty Ltd

10 9 8 7 6 5 4 3 2 1

For my family

Acknowledgements

I owe much to my parents Ian and Jan Hay for choosing to live in a special and remote part of Western Australia. This book could not have been written without the help of John Cahill who accompanied me on my trips to Middle Island.

CSIRO's Dr Peter Shaughnessy and Dr Nick Gales, who is now with the Australian Antarctic Division, shared their knowledge of sea lions and fur seals on a research trip to Kangaroo Island. Malcolm Traill and Julia Mitchell from the Local Studies Section of the Albany Library were always helpful in their responses to my numerous enquiries.

My thanks to Marcella Pollain and Dr Brenda Walker of the University of Western Australia's creative writing program for getting me started and Brenda for reading my completed manuscript.

Thanks to my grandmother Nancy Hay who read my chapters as they were written and for her belief in my work; my friends Kerry and Garry Walker for our Friday night discussions that helped me discover what I wanted to say; my husband Jamie Venerys for his support; Chris and Christine Bradley; Jill Bear; Stephen and Dorothy Purdew; and my son Robert for being there.